"Hi, Mr. Mathews," Maria said. "Is Ken there?"

"No, he's out," he responded.

Maria shot a glance at the clock, checking to make sure she hadn't read the digital numbers wrong. Ken was *not* a morning person.

"Where'd he go?" she blurted out.

"Well, a bunch of cheerleaders came by pretty early this morning," Mr. Mathews said. "And I haven't seen him since a little after nine . . ."

He never actually said that Ken left with the cheerleaders, she told herself. Mr. Matthews was annoyed because Maria had called him on the way he'd been treating Ken, so now he was trying to turn her into an insecure nutcase. That way Ken wouldn't have to dump her for another girl—she'd push him away all on her own. The guy's plan wasn't hard to see through. She just had to make sure she didn't let it work.

Don't miss any of the books in SWEET VALLEY HIGH SENIOR YEAR, an exciting series from Bantam Books!

Visit the Official Sweet Valley Web Site on the Internet at:

www.sweetvalley.com

Pascal's
senioryear

DATE DUE

APR 8 2006			
JUN 2 2 2007			
7-3-08			

BANTAM BOOKS
NEW YORK · TORONTO · LONDON · SYDNEY · AUCKLAND

RL: 6, AGES 012 AND UP

THE IT GUY

A Bantam Book / September 2000

Sweet Valley High® is a registered trademark of Francine Pascal.
Conceived by Francine Pascal.
Cover photography by Michael Segal.

Copyright © 2000 by Francine Pascal.
Cover art copyright © 2000 by 17th Street Productions,
an Alloy Online, Inc. company.

Produced by 17th Street Productions,
an Alloy Online, Inc. company.
33 West 17th Street
New York, NY 10011.

ISBN: 0-553-49337-X

Visit us on the Web! www.randomhouse.com/teens

Published simultaneously in the United States and Canada

Bantam Books is an imprint of Random House Children's Books, a
division of Random House, Inc. BANTAM BOOKS and the rooster
colophon are registered trademarks of Random House, Inc. Bantam Books,
1540 Broadway, New York, New York 10036.

PRINTED IN THE UNITED STATES OF AMERICA

OPM   0 9 8 7 6 5 4 3 2 1

To Diana McNelis

Ken Matthews

When I first saw <u>Forrest Gump,</u> I thought it was a pretty stupid movie. I just didn't buy the way everything always worked out for Forrest. But I keep hearing that one silly line in my head, the one about life being like a box of chocolates because "you never know what you're gonna get."

I mean, one day you're sitting on the bench behind a first-string quarterback, feeling like your football career is over forever. And then—just like that—the next day you get this dark chocolate truffle thrown at you, and you <u>are</u> the star quarterback. So maybe Forrest wasn't totally off base.

Conner McDermott

When it comes down to it, life is really just a bunch of people wanting to talk about your problems. The locked door, the Walkman, and the answering machine are a lot more useful than friends.

Jade Wu

I was watching this biography on Madonna the other day, and it made me remember why I like her so much. She knew she wasn't the most beautiful one out there, the best dancer, the best songwriter, or even the best singer. But she wanted to be a major music star, so she focused on exactly what would get her there. She worked on her dancing, had lyrics written for her, took singing lessons, and sold herself as a sex symbol.

I'm not saying I'm the next Madonna or anything, but I do know how to get what I want. Life's a game, and you just have to learn how to play it right.

CHAPTER 1
Under Pressure

The second Ken Matthews opened his eyes on Sunday morning, he felt a burst of happiness surge through him. He blinked, trying to remember what he'd been dreaming about.

Then it hit him—this feeling had nothing to do with a dream. Ken sat up, untangling his legs from the dark blue sheets. The reason he felt more *alive* than he had in months was that last night he'd been back where he belonged. Will Simmons had been taken out of the SVH football game with an injury, and Ken had replaced him, scoring a touchdown that made the fans go crazy.

Smiling at the memory, he stretched out his arms, relishing the intense ache in his muscles. He closed his eyes again, replaying all the cheers and screams from the game in his head.

Suddenly the imaginary noises were interrupted by the sound of a car door slamming. Ken stretched his legs, then walked over to peek outside his window. A bright red convertible was parked at the end of the driveway, and a group of girls were clustered around his front door, bending over the welcome mat.

What are they doing? he wondered, squinting to get a closer look. They stood, and he saw they'd left something on his stoop. He turned his focus back to the girls and recognized four members of the SVH cheerleading squad: Jessica Wakefield, Lila Fowler, Annie Whitman, and Renee Talbot.

While he watched, the girls ran back over to the car and piled in. They honked once, then took off down the street.

That's right, Ken realized as he searched the floor for a shirt to throw on before heading downstairs. The cheerleaders had probably left him a spirit package. It was a tradition at SVH after a really exciting football victory. Ken had received a bunch of good stuff his junior year, when *he* was the star quarterback. It was weird how easily he'd forgotten something that used to be such a regular part of his life.

Maybe because this still doesn't feel real, he thought as he headed downstairs. He shook his head, hurrying through the hall toward his front door. It was hard to believe that last night *hadn't* been a dream. He'd imagined that moment a million times in the past couple of months, and then he'd barely been able to process when it was actually happening.

He reached the door and pulled it open, then

squatted to pick up the basket left by the cheerleaders. He grinned as he spotted a couple of chocolate bars, making a mental note to tell the cheerleaders that these spirit things actually *worked*. The sight of the treats, along with the note on top saying, *Ken Matthews is the man under pressure,* really made him want to get back on that field.

Ken shut the door and strolled into the kitchen. He dropped the basket down on the black Formica table and sank into a chair. Sunlight streamed through the window onto the table, making the edges almost shine. He leaned back and rested his hands behind his head. *Wow, this . . .*

"Feels good, doesn't it?"

Ken sat up straight, almost knocking over his chair. He turned and saw his dad standing in the doorway, wearing his blue terry-cloth bathrobe.

"Yeah, I guess," Ken muttered, feeling his good mood dissipate. He'd forgotten that he'd have to face his dad. It was funny—he'd waited so long for his dad to be proud of him, excited to talk to him, but now the idea made him feel almost sick.

"You guess?" Mr. Matthews shot back, his thick eyebrows arching. "Ken, you were amazing last night. After you flubbed the first play, I mean."

Ken cringed. Leave it to his dad to remember that part, even though his next play had been incredible.

"What's that? Spirit basket?" Mr. Matthews

asked, walking over to the table. He started digging through the basket, pulling out some candy. "They gave you the primo stuff," he said. The pride in his dad's voice was so obvious, Ken swallowed back a bad taste in his mouth. It took a bunch of chocolate bars to make his dad think he was worth something as a son?

"You have to admit," Mr. Matthews said, plopping down across from Ken, "it's got to feel good to be back on top." His light blue eyes gleamed with excitement. "The sound of the crowd cheering, cheerleaders dropping off treats, your name in the headlines of the sports section . . ."

Ken blinked. His dad was the sportswriter covering the game last night. So if there was a big article on him in the *Tribune,* then Mr. Matthews was the one who wrote it. Ken couldn't help feeling a twinge of happiness. After all those harsh comments about what a loser his son was, Mr. Matthews had finally written something glowing for everyone in Sweet Valley to read. But the triumph disappeared as Ken immediately reminded himself that his dad had tried to get out of covering the game in the first place when he thought Ken would be on the bench, like usual.

"Hate to say it," Mr. Matthews went on, shaking his head. "But it sure was a stroke of luck that Simmons got that injury. He was playing with so much confidence that you would have finished your high-school career without another huddle." He paused, then looked Ken right in the eye. "The world works in funny ways, huh?"

Ken felt his stomach twist. He didn't want to think about the fact that his big moment had come at Will's expense. Not that Ken was a major fan of the guy, but being taken out on a stretcher had to have been pretty awful.

"It looked bad," Mr. Matthews said. He stood and crossed over to the refrigerator, pulling out a carton of orange juice. "I wouldn't be surprised if the kid's out for the season," he added over his shoulder.

Ken's heart sped up, and a million thoughts raced through his head. That would mean that Ken would have his position back—permanently.

It would also mean that Will Simmons's future would be destroyed. Was Ken a total jerk for hoping that his dad could be right?

He ran a hand through his short blond hair, trying to keep himself together. He had to get out of here, away from his dad. He had to think.

"I've gotta get going," Ken blurted out, jumping up from his chair. "I have some stuff to do."

"On Sunday, after a game night?" Mr. Matthews asked, his forehead creasing. "Aren't you supposed to relax today?"

"Wish I could," Ken said, avoiding his dad's gaze. "But I've got, um, a paper. I need to get to the library for research." The need to leave his house was getting stronger every second, and he practically ran out of the kitchen.

Last night had been *his* victory, not his dad's—and he was going to make sure that was very clear.

"I can't believe Todd's dad answered the door in his *underwear*," Jessica said, rolling her eyes. She just wished her sister could have been there to see her ex-boyfriend's father in his skivvies.

She's going to die when I tell her, Jessica thought. She held House of Java's front door open for Annie, Lila, and Renee, then followed them inside.

"That *was* scary," Lila agreed, flipping her long, brown hair back over her shoulder. "I think the rest of the squad will be happy they missed it."

The rest of the squad. As if Melissa and her crew would have come along on the spirit run anyway, even if Will hadn't been injured last night. Tia had begged off, claiming she desperately needed to catch up on sleep. Jessica had been surprised that Lila wanted to join in. She'd invited her to be nice since Lila had been slightly less obnoxious to her lately, but without Tia around, the two of them had been joking around in the car like they used to. It was definitely weird—but not bad.

"So what do you guys want to drink?" Jessica asked, heading over to the counter, where Corey, one of her least-favorite coworkers, was busy rearranging the coffee filters.

6

Corey looked up at them and frowned, her black-rimmed eyes narrowing into slits. "You guys are way too happy for this early in the morning," she said.

"Can I get a caramel latte?" Lila asked. "With skim milk, please."

Jessica smirked. She and Jeremy always used to make fun of customers who ordered lattes without real milk. Totally missing the point. It was a very Lila Fowler thing to do.

Annie and Renee placed their orders, then Jessica asked for a cup of chai tea, and they all walked back to the red, puffy, couchlike booth in the corner. As soon as Jessica sat down, she scanned the coffee shop. It was hard to be there and not feel like she was on duty, even when it wasn't her shift.

Sunday morning was always a strange crowd. Old guy at table three, sipping his water and mumbling to himself. Professional-looking businesswoman pecking at her laptop at table six. And . . . ooh. Cute twenty-something guy in a suit, reading a novel, at table twelve.

"Don't you love the way guys look in suits?" Lila said, practically on cue.

Jessica grinned. She crossed one leg over the other, yanking down her knee-length skirt at the same time. She'd never seen Jeremy in a suit, but she could picture how good he would look. . . .

Feeling a blush creep over her cheeks, she quickly

7

stopped herself from coming up with a mental image. She just couldn't get Jeremy out of her head now that she knew he and Jade were over. She finally had the chance to fix the huge mistake she'd made when she chose Will.

"So why didn't Jade come?" Annie asked, leaning across the small, round table.

Jessica flinched. Exactly the question she'd been hoping to avoid. *Because she wasn't invited,* she thought. Being around Jade at the game last night had been hard enough, knowing she had to fire her. Jessica had been going over it in her head a million times, trying to figure out how to break the news. But no matter what, she knew Jade was going to totally lose it on her.

"Your drinks are ready," Corey said as she passed by on her way to drop something off at a nearby table.

Jessica jumped up, happy for the excuse to avoid Annie's question. She was used to Corey's laziness, and this time it was actually useful. "I'll go get them," she said quickly, already moving toward the counter.

"Jessica, you're early," a familiar voice called out right as she was reaching for the tray of drinks.

Jessica whirled around, coming face-to-face with Ally Scott, House of Java's manager. Ally's straight, brown hair was messier than usual, and her zippered sweatshirt seemed a little off center.

"Hi, Ally," Jessica said, flashing her a grin. "I'm here with my friends, actually. My shift doesn't start until—"

"I'm glad you're here," Ally interrupted. She took a few steps closer. "I wanted to talk to you before you start your shift anyway."

Jessica glanced back and forth between the drinks and her boss, frowning.

"It'll only take a minute," Ally promised.

"Let me just drop these off," Jessica said, grabbing the tray. She strode over to her friends' booth and placed the drinks down in front of them. "I'll be right back," she said, turning to go talk to Ally.

Maybe this will have nothing to do with Jade, she told herself, aware that it was a total lie.

"So what's up?" she asked Ally, following her over to a spot by the wall near the big oil painting of a woman drinking coffee.

Ally folded her arms over her chest and fixed Jessica with one of her dead-on stares. "I just wanted to give you a heads up," she began. "I told Jade to drop by this afternoon during your shift."

Jessica took in a quick breath, then leaned against the wall for support. Today? She had to fire Jade today?

"Just tell her everything we talked about yesterday," Ally continued. "Calling in sick at the last minute and then showing up here as a customer

9

that same night is not acceptable. And neither is her attitude."

And if I say that, she'll know exactly who told Ally, Jessica thought. She'd been the one who was there that night, not Ally. Jade was tough—if she was out for revenge, Jessica had a feeling it wouldn't be fun.

Just focus on Jeremy, Jessica told herself, trying to slow down her breathing. She'd gone to Ally with the info as a last-ditch effort to keep her from letting Jeremy quit. Once the ugly part was over—the part where she fired Jade and Jade went ballistic—Jessica could tell Jeremy he didn't need to leave, and then once they were working side by side again, things would go back to the way they used to be.

"So you're okay with this?" Ally asked, eyeing Jessica closely.

She smiled. "I'm all set."

Maria Slater sat straight up in bed, beads of sweat on her forehead.

Relax, Maria. It was just a nightmare, she reassured herself, taking a deep breath. It wasn't the first bad dream she'd had last night. The little sleep she'd actually gotten had been filled with scary images of a wrecked relationship with Ken. In this dream she'd been invisible. Well, not entirely invisible. Some people could see her, like Elizabeth and her mom. But Ken . . . he looked right through her.

Maria groaned. She couldn't believe she was actually taking Ken's dad's stupid comment about all the girls who'd be after Ken now so seriously. Okay, so maybe the girls in the stands *did* go crazy when Ken scored the touchdown, but it wasn't like Ken asked for that. And even if he'd had his one night back in the spotlight, he was still the guy she trusted, the guy who'd been there for her so many times this year.

She let out a deep sigh, then dropped her head back into the pillows. Mr. Matthews wanted his son to be a big football star—probably with a cheerleader girlfriend to match. He'd never talked much to Maria, and she was clear on the fact that she wasn't his ideal choice for Ken. But that hadn't kept them apart so far.

Ken can't even stand to be around his dad, Maria told herself. She stared up at her stucco ceiling, concentrating on getting her breathing under control. Mr. Matthews was a real jerk who'd made his son feel like dirt when he was stuck on the bench. So just because *he* wasn't going to be around to enjoy Ken's victory didn't mean Maria wouldn't be.

I should give him a call, she decided. She'd never had the chance to congratulate him last night since he went out with the guys on the team after the game. She searched the room for her blue cordless phone, spotting it on top of her dresser. In a second she was across the room with the phone in her hand, dialing Ken's number.

It rang once, and Maria glanced over at the clock by her bed. Was nine forty-five too early to call on a Sunday morning after a game?

He won't mind, she thought. He would probably be psyched to know she was thinking about him.

"Hello?"

Maria froze. She hadn't even considered the possibility that Mr. Matthews would answer. She stared down at the tantalizing phone button. *I could always hang up and call back later. . . .*

"Hello? Anyone there?"

Maria cleared her throat. "Hi, sorry. Is Ken there?"

"No, he's out," Mr. Matthews responded.

Maria shot another glance at the clock, checking to make sure she hadn't read the digital numbers wrong. Ken was *not* a morning person.

"Where'd he go?" she blurted out.

"I'm not sure," Mr. Matthews said. He paused, and Maria traced the edge of her dresser with her fingers, wondering what to say next.

"Well, a bunch of cheerleaders came by pretty early this morning," he added. "And I haven't seen him since a little after nine . . ."

What was *that* supposed to mean? She held the receiver away from her ear, hoping he hadn't heard the little sound that escaped her mouth.

He's just trying to get to you. Don't let him.

"Oh, okay. Could you just tell him I called, then?" she asked, sinking down onto her plush carpet.

"Sure. Who's calling again?"

You know who this is. The guy was an even bigger jerk than she'd realized. "It's Maria," she said coldly.

"Right. Good to talk to you, Maria. I'll have Ken call you later."

He hung up, and Maria threw the phone onto her bed, then pulled her knees to her chest, resting her chin on them.

He never actually said that Ken left with the cheerleaders. Mr. Matthews was annoyed because Maria had called him on the way he'd been treating Ken, so now he was trying to turn her into an insecure nutcase. That way Ken wouldn't have to dump her for another girl—she'd push him away all on her own. The guy's plan wasn't hard to see through. She just had to make sure she didn't let it work.

Conner McDermott

The Temple of Pound

A pulsing throb of insanity,
Consuming my mind—
An endless vault of pain.
Unrelenting,
Uncaring,
Yet giving companion,
Sharing its tainted gift of torture.

CHAPTER 2

Serious Danger

Ken creaked open the front door of his house and stepped inside, peering around the hallway. *Good.* His dad was nowhere in sight. But the cordless phone was. Ken could see it on the table right by the entrance to the living room.

He groaned. He needed that phone to call Maria from his bedroom, where he could shut the door. Unfortunately, it was in the Red Zone. Chances were that right now his father was sitting on the living-room sofa, reading the Sunday paper.

If he timed it right, he could grab the phone while his dad was engrossed in some sports column and then dash up the stairs before being caught in a conversation. Ken slipped off his sneakers and walked quietly down the hall. With one quick motion he reached for the phone and then spun around and headed upstairs.

He was on his way into his room when the phone rang in his hand, giving him a start.

He brought the phone up to his ear and clicked it on. "Yeah," he said, breathless. "Hello?"

"Ken? Didn't you get my message? I was calling back to see if your dad knew when you'd be home."

He frowned. "No, I just walked in the door. But I was about to call you. What's wrong?" His usually chill girlfriend sounded *very* tense, and he'd expected her to be happy when they finally talked, excited about last night.

"No, I'm fine," she said. "I was just wondering where you went so early. Your dad, um, said something about cheerleaders?"

Ending a sentence on that up note was not like Maria. Something was definitely wrong. Ken strode into his room and shut the door behind him, then flopped down on his bed, pushing aside his plaid bedspread.

"I had to get out of the house," he explained. "My dad was bugging me. So I went to the library and did some reading. But I really wanted to talk to you, so I came back here to give you a call." There—that should make her happy, right?

"And the . . . cheerleaders?" she asked, the strange squeak in her voice not going away.

"Oh, right," he said, letting out a small sigh. "They dropped off a spirit basket because of my touchdown last night." *The one you haven't congratulated me on yet,* he added silently. Maybe it was petty, but he would have expected her to show a little more enthusiasm after what a big deal the game had been for him.

"That was nice," she said stiffly. "So, why was your dad bothering you? He was so into you last night."

"Yeah, I know," Ken said. "He's gushing with pride for Ken the Fearless Quarterback. But after not noticing me for the last couple of months, I don't really want to deal."

"Yeah, I actually talked to him last night, and he—"

The call waiting beeped, drowning out the end of Maria's sentence.

". . . really strange," Maria continued after the beep. "Then when I called before, he—"

Another beep cut off that sentence too. Ken knew Maria wasn't in a great mood, and interrupting her probably wouldn't make it better. But the beeping wouldn't stop, and it could be someone important for his dad.

"Maria, I'm sorry," he said. "I have another call. Can you hold on just a sec?"

Maria paused. "Yeah, sure," she replied quietly.

"I'll be right back," he promised before clicking over to the other line.

"Hello?" he answered.

"Matthews," a gruff voice said. "It's Coach."

Ken felt his neck muscles tighten. He had associated his football coach with nothing but bad news for months. *Ease up,* he told himself. After last night's game things were different. Hopefully.

"Hey, Coach," he said, fiddling with his gray pillowcase.

17

"Listen, Matthews, I just want you to know that Will Simmons is out for the season. You're our man now."

Out for the season. Whoa. Ken had seen Will grimacing in pain as the stretcher took him off the field, but that didn't necessarily mean . . .

Ken felt the same rush of mixed emotions he'd experienced talking to his dad earlier. Sympathy for Will but also incredible excitement. Starting quarterback. The position was his again.

"Is Will okay?" he asked, trying not to seem too psyched under the circumstances.

"He will be," Coach Riley said. "He went through emergency surgery last night. I gave the hospital a buzz today to check on his condition, and basically the injury's extensive enough that he won't be back on that field anytime soon, if ever."

If ever? The words echoed in Ken's head as he imagined what they would do to Will when he heard them. It was one thing sitting on the bench because you went through a rough patch and quit the team. But not being physically able to play—that was another story. A bad one.

"Listen, you have to focus on the team right now," Coach Riley continued. "Will's got his family looking out for him. But you've got big shoes to fill, Matthews. You're going to have to start training your butt off. I expect you to be the first one to practice, the last one to leave. And you've gotta be more vocal—on and *off* the field. Will turned himself into a hell of a leader, and I need you to do the same, to pull these guys through this."

"You can count on me," Ken said, realizing how much responsibility this was. It wasn't just about playing well—it was about rallying a team around him midseason, when they'd all learned to trust a different quarterback and watched that guy taken away on a stretcher.

"I don't have to tell you that this is a great opportunity," Coach said. "We're one of the toughest teams in the state right now. If we stay in this position, you might even be looking at a scholarship."

A scholarship? Ken sat up, dropping the pillow he'd been turning over in his hand. This was amazing. Maria would be . . .

Shoot—Maria. She was probably pretty annoyed right now. At least he'd never heard the click that meant she'd hung up on the other line.

"You've got a strong arm and a good sense for the game. Now all you need is to step up the confidence," Coach Riley said. Ken found himself nodding. "Are you ready for the challenge?"

"Definitely," Ken said, pressing his lips together.

"That's what I like to hear," Coach said. "I'll talk to you more tomorrow before practice. Get some rest."

"Will do."

"Bye, Matthews."

As soon as he heard the click, Ken switched back over to his other line. "Maria?" he said, hoping she wasn't too mad. "Hello?"

Silence. Ken's pulse quickened.

"Are you still there?" he asked, even though she had to be—or he'd be listening to a dial tone right now.

"Yeah," Maria finally responded. "I guess I just dozed off for a second while I was waiting."

"Sorry," Ken said, ignoring the razors in her voice. "But that was Coach Riley. You're not going to believe this—Will's out for the season. I mean, I know that sucks for him—but I'm going to have my position back. Coach started in on this pep talk, and I couldn't cut him off, not when he needs to know I'm totally committed."

"So you're starting quarterback again?" Maria asked in a strange, emotionless tone. "Wow, that's— so I guess you're really happy."

"Yeah, I am," he said, suddenly feeling awkward. He'd been so pumped to share the news with her, especially the chance of getting a scholarship. But it didn't sound like she even cared.

Of course she cares. Maria was the most caring person he knew. She was just in a bad mood.

"Before I forget," she began, "there's something I wanted to tell you."

Ken grinned. Here it was—the praise for last night he'd been expecting.

"It's about Conner," she went on, causing his smile to fade as quickly as it had come. Conner? What did her ex have to do with anything?

"Oh, yeah?" he said, narrowing his eyes in annoyance.

"Remember that crazy scene at The Shack after his show Friday night?" Maria asked, completely missing Ken's obvious lack of interest. "Well, Liz told me he's been a wreck all weekend. He fell off the rocks at Crescent Beach because he was so wasted, and he's been pushing Liz away since then."

Okay, based on what Ken knew about Conner— which wasn't much—it wasn't exactly bizarre behavior to push his girlfriend away. And maybe he had a little too much to drink the other night, but that happened sometimes.

"Isn't that terrible?" Maria pressed when he didn't say anything.

"I don't know," he said. He stood and walked over to his desk, picking up a paper clip and twisting the metal around. "I don't really know Conner that well."

"Well," Maria said, "Elizabeth's really worried."

"Maybe he's just going through a rough period," Ken said. The paper clip was totally bent out now, one long, thin line.

"No, that's just it; his life's been going really well. His mom is sober, he's been getting music gigs, and his—"

Call waiting . . . again. This time it was almost a relief—a break from hearing about poor Conner.

"Sorry," Ken said, "but that's the other line again. I'll be right back." He clicked over before she could protest. "Hello?"

"Matthews. What's up, man?"

Ken recognized Todd Wilkins's voice. They used to talk all the time, even though they hadn't been that close this year. "Hey, Todd. Do you mind if I call you right—"

"I just have a quick question," Todd interrupted. "What are you doing Wednesday night?"

"Nothing, I don't think."

"Great," Todd said. "Because I talked to a couple of guys from the team today after we found out about Simmons. We're gonna have a team party Wednesday night, and you're the main event." Todd chuckled. "We're gonna properly initiate you to your new role, if you get my drift."

Ken sat down on his desk chair, leaning back. Ever since the earthquake he hadn't been that into the party thing, but now that he was starting quarterback again, he should probably go just to show his team spirit. Coach Riley had told him that he needed to be a leader both on and *off* the field. That included stuff like team parties . . . right?

"Yeah, fine, I'll be there," he said.

"Cool. Later, Matthews. And good game last night."

"Thanks. Bye."

Ken clicked back over. "Hello?"

Silence. Again. Maria was *really* touchy today. Was it all because she was worried about Conner? Even when Ken had so much going on in his life?

"That was Todd," he said. He was about to tell her about the party, but somehow it just didn't seem like she'd want to hear it. "So, what were you saying about Conner?"

"Were you even listening?" Maria snapped.

Ken opened his mouth, then let it close again when nothing came out. He didn't know what to say.

"I'm sorry," she said quickly. "I'm just . . . hungry, I guess. I can tell you about Conner later. I think I need to get something to eat."

Ken felt his jaw tighten. He knew he'd been rude, putting her on hold for a while when he talked to his coach, but after this whole conversation she *still* hadn't said anything about how he played last night.

"I really should go," she said. "I have a lot of work. But that's great about your position. You've already got tons of fans, so they'll probably be thrilled."

Ken frowned. What did that mean? The only fan he cared about was her—and she didn't seem to realize anything had even *happened*.

"Okay, I guess I'll see you tomorrow," he told her. "I hope you feel better. After you eat, I mean."

"Thanks," she said. "Bye."

Ken hung up, wishing he knew what her problem

was. He was truly happy for the first time in so long—so why wasn't she happy *for* him?

Conner McDermott lay on his bed in a T-shirt and boxer shorts, with the shades pulled tight and vintage Santana playing softly in the background. He had created a perfectly contained, low-maintenance environment in which to avoid the world . . . and nurse The Headache.

Lifting his fingertips to his temples, he started rubbing in a circular motion like he'd seen his mom do before. But it wasn't working. Instead it felt like his fingertips were sending lightning bolts straight into his brain.

Maybe I should just let the music relax me, he thought, dropping his hands from his head. He wondered if he'd ever be able to play on this level. Probably not, but it was a nice thought.

Conner shut his eyes and focused on the notes, shutting out the sensation of pain. If it weren't for music, he wasn't sure what else would be worth it. School was pretty much a waste. The only class he could take seriously was creative writing, and even then he had to deal with Elizabeth's worried glances and the effect her amazing blue-green eyes had on him. . . .

A loud knock on the door interrupted his thoughts. He grabbed his stereo remote and hit the mute button. Time to play dead.

"Conner?"

His mom. Right there in the top-five people he didn't want to deal with.

"I really need to talk to you, Conner. It will just take a second."

A second in Mom time was longer than he felt like being around anyone. But if he ignored her, she would just keep bugging him. Maybe he could get this over with and spend the rest of the day sleeping. "Come in," he said.

The door opened, and Mrs. Sandborn slipped inside. Before saying a word, she opened the blinds completely, filling his room with harsh brightness. Conner blinked, then focused in on her. She looked pretty pale, and her long, blond hair was pulled back into a messy ponytail with strands falling over her cheeks. Even when she used to be drunk all the time, she would always present a neat appearance.

"I just wanted to be able to see you," his mom said, squinting to get a good look. Instinctively Conner sank down lower on his bed, shrinking from her gaze.

She stood there for a moment, rubbing her palms along the sides of her faded jeans. Then she took a step closer, clenching and unclenching her fists.

"What is it?" Conner barked. He wasn't in the mood to watch her little display of uncomfortable I-have-no-clue-how-to-talk-to-my-own-son actions.

"I know this may be difficult coming from me, of

all people," Mrs. Sandborn said, taking another small step forward. "But I feel like—well, if . . . it's just that—"

"What?" Conner interrupted, raking his hand through his hair. "Let's get this over with."

Her shoulders drooped, and her tense features tightened even more. He knew he should feel bad about reducing her to this state. But something about that vulnerable look, that slump in her shoulders, only angered him. It was so desperate, so hypocritical of her to accuse him of anything.

"I know I've already said this," she stated, "but you have to listen to me. You have a problem." She paused, and he held back a groan as he anticipated her next words. "*A drinking problem.*"

Conner's skin felt hot, and anger coursed through his veins. She was so pathetically predictable. "You think so?" he asked, turning away to stare at his wall.

"Yes," she said. She came over and perched on the edge of his bed. He could smell a faint whiff of her flowery perfume. It was familiar but also not— since it always used to be mingled with the scent of alcohol when he got near her. Only now it was just flowers.

"You're acting crazy, pushing people away, pushing *me* away—it's not healthy, Conner. You're heading for serious danger."

He snorted, unable to take her preachy little act.

After everything she'd put him through when she was a full-on alcoholic, she had the nerve to try and accuse *him*. He was the one who'd held their family together all those years while she was out getting drunk.

"I know what you're thinking," she continued, her voice growing steadier, more solid. "You can handle it. You can stop anytime you want. Well, you're wrong." She reached out and put her hand under his chin, moving his face so that she could look right into his eyes. Her fingers were cold against his skin. "I also know what you feel right now. Your mouth is dry, no matter how much water you drink. Your head is pounding, and your stomach is a wreck."

My stomach's fine, he thought. *Except this little show of yours is making me pretty sick.* He wrenched himself out of her grasp, then threw his legs over the side of the bed and stood up. A wave of dizziness came over him, but he ignored it and strolled as calmly as possible past his mom to his bedroom door. He grabbed the handle and pulled it open. Then, with a quick glance toward his mom and a flick of the wrist, he motioned for her to leave.

"You want me to leave?" Mrs. Sandborn asked. "Fine. But I'll be back. I'm not letting you go through this alone." She got up and brushed by him, then he heard her footsteps going down the stairs.

He slammed his door shut and turned the lock to avoid further disturbances.

Crashing back down on his bed, Conner reached out and punched one of his pillows, which barely put a dent in his frustration. His mom was calling him an alcoholic. A drunk. How long had she been out of the rehab clinic? And her first move as a responsible mom was to tell him that he had a *problem*.

He looked up from his mattress and searched for the stereo remote, turning the volume back up until the music drowned out everything else.

Who wouldn't need a drink with all these hysterical women running around with sad faces? A few drinks here and there wasn't alcoholism. It was survival.

In fact, right now it would really do him some good. Conner reached under his bed, feeling around blindly until his fingers made contact with the bottle. He pulled it out and stared at the brownish liquid for a moment, a small smile coming to his lips. Then he took a swig, letting the scotch glide down his throat, filling him with soothing, blissful relief.

I should be paid extra for this, Jessica thought, her gaze fixed directly on the door to House of Java from her position behind the counter. Firing someone was *not* in her job description. Okay, so maybe it was now that she was an assistant manager—but still, firing someone she knew? Someone she went to school with and cheered with? It definitely called for a bonus.

The door started to open, and Jessica straightened, holding her breath as she waited. *Please don't be Jade.*

And . . . it wasn't. Unless Jade had dyed her hair blond and aged about twenty years.

Jessica exhaled, her mouth forming a fake, pleasant smile for the customer. She was beginning to understand why businessmen always had ulcers and heart trouble. Laying someone off was already giving her an ulcer . . . and she hadn't even done it yet.

"Welcome to House of Java—may I help you?" she said on autopilot as the woman approached her.

"Um . . . yes," the woman muttered, glancing behind Jessica at the big menu board with drinks and prices listed in bold print. "Do you have those steamed milk drinks with flavors?"

"Yes, we do," Jessica said. "The flavors are listed up there," she added, pointing at the right spot on the menu board. "We have raspberry, crème de menthe, vanilla—" Jessica heard the door jingle and stopped, turning her attention back to the door. *Please don't be . . .*

It was Jade. As usual, she was hard to miss—even if Jessica hadn't been watching for her. She was wearing a tight, V-necked white shirt with a supershort red skirt and strappy, high-heel sandals. Her eyes locked with Jessica's, and she headed straight toward her, her hips swaying as she stepped.

"Miss?"

Jessica snapped back to attention, looking at the customer.

"I'd like the vanilla steamed milk, please," the woman said, a hint of annoyance in her voice.

Jessica rang up the order, keeping Jade in her peripheral vision the whole time. "I'll bring you the drink when it's ready," she said. "You can go sit down if you want."

As soon as the woman walked away, Jade stepped up to the counter, leaning her elbows on the surface. "Would you mind telling me why I'm here?" she asked. "I'd rather not spend one extra second around you than absolutely necessary."

This might be easier than I thought. Jessica had hoped that Jade would be her usual semibitchy self, to keep the guilt factor low. But no matter what, Jade was going to take this as an outright declaration of war. Jade would definitely strike back—on the cheerleading team, at school, with Jeremy.

Jeremy.

Jade would think this was all about Jeremy—which it *totally* wasn't. Well, maybe a little. But only because Jessica wanted Jeremy to come back to HOJ. And he was a much better worker than Jade was anyway. Jessica *hadn't* been lying when she'd told Ally all the stuff Jade was doing wrong.

Jessica pulled the metal milk container away from the steamer and added a squirt of vanilla syrup to a mug. As she poured the frothy milk into the mug, she noticed both hands were shaking.

You've got to chill out. It was her job as assistant manager to deal with the staff. Jade would have to understand that this was nothing personal. It was Ally's idea, and Jessica simply had to carry out the order.

"Actually, Ally wanted me to talk to you," Jessica said, studying the coffee grounds lying next to the espresso machine. "But let me just give that woman her drink first."

She delivered the steamed milk, her hands growing clammier by the second. As she walked back to the counter, she wiped her palms on her green apron, but they were already starting to sweat again by the time she reached Jade.

"So what is it that's so important?" Jade asked, tapping her sandal on the floor.

"Right," Jessica said, shifting her weight from one foot to the other. "Um, this is kind of hard," she began, still avoiding Jade's gaze. "Ally talked to me this morning, and I'm really sorry, but—" She stopped, finally looking directly at Jade, whose eyes were narrowed into small slits. Gathering her courage, Jessica blurted out, "You're fired."

There. She felt a spark of triumph at having gotten out the words, but it was immediately replaced by overwhelming uneasiness when she saw the expression of shock and indignation that came over Jade's features.

"I'm *what?*" Jade spat. She gave her head a little shake, tossing her shoulder-length black hair away from her face. "Do you want to tell me why?"

Jessica bit her lip. This was the part she'd really been dreading.

"I mean, there has to be some *reason*," Jade added. "This is totally out of the blue." Suddenly a strange light flickered in her eyes, and Jessica got a sick feeling in her stomach. "Except for the fact that I just broke up with Jeremy," she said.

Jessica's temper flared. "Ally wouldn't care about that," she said, her voice rising. She grabbed a napkin and started angrily wiping up the coffee grounds. "I think it was more the part where you skipped a shift, then showed up to rub it in my face."

Jade's mouth dropped open, then slowly closed again as her lips formed a taunting smile. "And how did Ally find out about that?" she asked, crossing her arms over her chest.

Jessica swallowed. She hadn't meant to let that information out, but Jade really knew how to get to her, make her lose control.

"I'm sure you had nothing to do with it," Jade said, still smirking. "It's a *total* coincidence that Ally randomly realized today—right after my breakup with Jeremy—that I had to be fired."

There was nothing to say—no way to defend herself. Jade had her.

"Just so you know, Jess, I won't forget this." Jade spun around and strode out of House of Java, leaving Jessica wondering exactly when—and how—she'd face the fallout from what she'd just done.

Conner McDermott

The Catch-22 of Denial

Here's the thing no one seems to get about "denial," as all the AA freaks call it. If someone accuses you of something, and they're dead wrong . . . what do you do? Deny it, right? But then they turn around and tell you that's a sign that they're right because you're in <u>denial</u>.

What a load.

CHAPTER
Out of My League
3

Jade slumped down into the driver's seat of her black Nissan and slammed the door shut, letting her head rest against the hot steering wheel.

Fired. Again. Twice in three weeks—that had to be some kind of record. At least First and Ten had let her go for an actual reason, though. Not just because some spoiled girl wanted revenge over a *guy*.

She couldn't believe that she used to think Jessica Wakefield was cool. The girl was so used to getting everything she wanted handed to her that she couldn't deal when Jeremy chose Jade over her. Her petty little stunt at the beach was one thing—dragging Jeremy along to catch Jade making out with Josh Radinsky. But taking her job away was beyond low.

Jade turned the key in the ignition so that she could put on the radio, but she didn't trust herself to go out on the road yet—she was afraid she'd ram right into a tree or something, imagining it was Jessica's face.

What was she going to do? She needed that job. Her mom counted on her contributing to stuff around the apartment. Worse, her jerk of a father would only send child support if Jade had a steady job—and her mom didn't have the time or money to go after him in court if he withheld the payments.

She glanced up at her reflection in the rearview mirror and winced at what she saw. Tears were gathering in her eyes, sending streaks of mascara running down her cheeks.

Pathetic. Was she going to let Jessica win like this? No way. That's not how she worked.

Taking a deep breath, Jade pulled out of the House of Java parking lot and onto the street, her hands clenching the steering wheel in a death grip.

Self-pity was a waste of time. She'd find another job—and she'd find a way to make Jessica regret this.

Just as Elizabeth settled into the sofa for an afternoon of mindless bad television, the doorbell rang. She sighed, tossing aside the throw pillow on her lap and heading for the front door.

Jessica was at work, and her parents were out running errands. But she wasn't expecting anyone.

Conner? Her heart jumped at the thought, even though she knew it was barely possible. Just in case, she stopped for a mirror check in the hall. Her hair was clean, just a little messy. She ran her fingers through it as she surveyed her outfit—jeans and an old SVJH T-shirt from junior high. Whatever—if Conner was actually standing on her doorstep after their fight yesterday, then he wouldn't care how she looked, and neither would she.

The doorbell rang again, and Elizabeth hurried to answer it. *It's not going to be him,* she told herself as she pulled open the door.

But her heart still dropped when she saw that she was right. It wasn't Conner. Instead Mrs. Sandborn stood there, giant bags under her light blue eyes. Elizabeth's breath caught as she took in the deep crease in Mrs. Sandborn's forehead. Something was wrong.

"I'm sorry to surprise you," Mrs. Sandborn said. "But I think we need to talk. Is this a bad time?"

"No, of course not," Elizabeth said, stepping back from the door. "Come on in."

She led her to the living room, then sat down on the love seat, waving a hand at the sofa for Mrs. Sandborn to make herself comfortable. Conner's mother had never been to her house before, and it felt strange to have her there, especially without Conner.

Pressing her hands into the soft material on either side of her, Elizabeth racked her brain for what to say to the woman she barely knew, who might be her only hope for helping Conner.

"Can I, um, get you something to drink?" she offered. She cringed immediately, wondering if that was a bad thing to say to a recovering alcoholic. "I mean, we have orange juice or soda," she added quickly. That probably just made it worse—like she was assuming Mrs. Sandborn would have asked for alcohol.

"I'm fine, thanks," Mrs. Sandborn assured her, luckily not seeming to notice her awkwardness. "Actually, I'm here to discuss what happened yesterday."

Elizabeth nodded, an image of Conner's bandaged arm coming into her mind, followed by the memory of the insults he'd hurled at her before running out of the house.

"He came home drunk again last night," Mrs. Sandborn continued, twisting her hands together in her lap. "Elizabeth, I'm pretty sure about this—I think my son is an alcoholic."

Even though she'd been expecting the words, Elizabeth's head jerked back involuntarily when she heard them out loud. She turned her gaze to the window, focusing on the neighbors' kids across the street. They were playing catch in their front yard. It was a regular Sunday routine for them. Predictable, reliable.

Conner's an alcoholic. . . . She'd been telling herself that he had a problem, a drinking problem, but she hadn't actually used that word for it yet. It seemed so final, so harsh and cold. And also so *foreign*—part of a world that she knew so little about.

She blinked, then looked back at Mrs. Sandborn, who was watching her with pleading eyes, as if there was something she could do or say that would make this whole thing go away.

Elizabeth took a shaky breath, realizing that she'd never felt so entirely helpless in her life. She cleared her throat. "So . . . what's next?" she managed to get out.

Mrs. Sandborn shook her head. "It's not going to be easy. I tried to confront him this morning, and he's not willing to listen. Which isn't surprising, really." She paused, staring down at her fingers as she eased her thin silver ring back and forth over her knuckle. "The experts say you have to let the person hit bottom—that the only person who can save you is yourself. And in my case, that was true." She raised her eyes back up to meet Elizabeth's. "But this is my son, and I can't just watch him destroy himself."

Elizabeth swallowed, terrified by the intensity of Mrs. Sandborn's expression.

"So the other option is to try an intervention," she stated, finally letting go of her ring.

"Okay," Elizabeth replied, licking her lips nervously. She'd heard the word before, but she wasn't really sure what it meant. This disease had a whole *vocabulary* she didn't know. How was she going to be any use to Conner at all?

Mrs. Sandborn reached out and laid her hand on Elizabeth's arm, giving her a gentle squeeze. "An intervention is when the person is confronted at once by a group of concerned friends and family. The idea is that an alcoholic will have a much harder time avoiding the truth when he's surrounded by everyone he cares about and they're all telling him the same thing."

"So, like, an *ambush?*" Elizabeth blurted out. That sounded like the last thing that Conner would respond to.

Mrs. Sandborn sighed. She let go of Elizabeth's arm and leaned back against the sofa. "I know it sounds scary," she said. "But it's really the only way we can get through to him at this point. You just have to trust me—this is something I know a lot about, unfortunately. A lot of people in rehab said they ended up there soon after interventions."

What am I supposed to say? Conner's mom *did* know much more about this than she did. But she knew Conner, and she couldn't imagine him sitting around to listen while all of his friends informed him that he was a . . . that he had a drinking problem. Just picturing the betrayed look on his face as he stepped into his living room and saw them there, waiting, was enough to make her shudder. He would never talk to her again.

"Elizabeth?" Mrs. Sandborn said, raising her eyebrows hopefully. "What do you think? Will you help me?"

Elizabeth took a deep breath, looking down at the carpet. Every instinct told her that this was a bad idea. But she was way out of her league here, so maybe her instincts weren't even relevant. Besides, she was being selfish—worrying about Conner hating her. The important thing was helping him, even if it meant he would be angry for a while—or even forever. She loved him, and she had to do whatever she could if he was really in danger.

"Yes," Elizabeth said. "I'll help. And I'll talk to the rest of his friends tomorrow, I promise."

Mrs. Sandborn's whole face relaxed. "Thank you, Elizabeth. This is very brave of you. And I'm relieved to know that Conner has someone so special in his life."

Elizabeth blushed. They barely knew each other—in fact, Mrs. Sandborn barely knew *Conner* after all the years of being sick. It felt wrong somehow for her to make a statement like that, even though it was something Elizabeth wanted so badly to believe was true.

"Okay, I should get going," Mrs. Sandborn said. They stood and headed over to the door. Before she left, Mrs. Sandborn took Elizabeth's hand in hers, gripping it so tightly that the ring she'd been playing with before pressed into Elizabeth's skin. "Let me know when you're all ready," she said.

"I will," Elizabeth replied, suddenly anxious for this to be over—to be alone again and have a chance to process everything.

Mrs. Sandborn tried to smile one last time, then

41

stepped outside, closing the door behind her.

I'm doing the right thing, Elizabeth told herself, hugging her arms around her chest as she leaned back against the heavy door. *Someday Conner will thank me.*

Someday in the very, very distant future.

Finally, Jessica thought with relief as she spotted Corey strolling back toward the counter. Her normally lazy coworker had somehow gotten the inspiration to clear off dishes from the tables in the back, but all Jessica wanted was for her to come up front so she could take her break—and call Jeremy.

"Can you cover me?" Jessica asked as soon as Corey got close.

Corey rolled her eyes. "I guess," she said in her usual disinterested tone. She pulled her apron tighter and stepped behind the counter, pressing herself against the wall to give Jessica room to get by.

"Thanks," Jessica said, giving Corey a quick shoulder pat as she passed her. Ever since Jade had stormed out, the only thing that had kept her from losing it big time was knowing that soon she could call Jeremy and tell him he was free to come back to work.

Jessica hurried into the employee lounge, going straight for the Princess phone on Ally's desk. She grabbed it and quickly dialed his number.

"Hello?"

Twinges of excitement surged through her at the sound of his voice. "Hey," she said, her face warming up with a deep blush. "It's me."

"Oh, hey, Jess," he said. "I'm sorry I didn't go to the game last night—I didn't get your e-mail until too late. What was it you wanted to tell me?"

A satisfied smile spread over her face. She'd been a little worried when he never showed up at the SVH football game, but of course he hadn't been purposely ignoring her. *Jeremy would never do that. Not to me.*

"Actually," Jessica said, cradling the phone close to her cheek, "I have some news."

Jeremy laughed—a warm, comforting sound. "I figured," he teased.

"Some *good* news," she explained, twirling the phone cord around her finger. "You don't have to quit. You can still work here!"

There was a long pause, and Jessica bit her lip, wondering why he wasn't saying anything. Wasn't this what he wanted?

"Jess, I already told you, I can't be there with—"

"No, you don't understand," she said quickly. "Jade was fired, so there's no problem. You won't have to deal with her at all."

"Wait a second—fired? Why?"

Jessica frowned. Did she really have to go through this again? And why did Jeremy *care* anyway? "Well, I mean . . . I don't know exactly," she lied.

43

"Ally just wasn't happy with her attitude, I guess. You know she wasn't the best worker in the world."

"Yeah, that's true," he said in a weird voice. "But I think she really needed this job. Is she okay?"

Excuse me? Since when did it matter if the girl who'd cheated on him was holding up all right? "I'm sure she's fine," Jessica replied through clenched teeth. This conversation was not going the way she'd planned.

"I can't believe Ally would just fire her like that," he continued. "Without giving her another chance or anything."

"I thought you would be *happy*," Jessica said, unable to keep the annoyance out of her voice. "Don't you get what this means? You have your job back. You don't have to quit now."

"I don't know," he said. "I was starting to think maybe a change would be good anyway. There's this new sushi restaurant opening up, and my dad knows the owner."

What? She'd been so confident that once she told him Jade was out of there, he'd be on his way over. *Time for a shift in technique,* she decided.

"Come on," she said in her best flirtatious tone. "I know you miss the jittery hands, the smell of roasting coffee beans. And how can you live without all the caffeine-addict freaks who sit here talking to themselves?"

That got a laugh. A good sign, she told herself.

All she had to do now was move in for the kill.

"Jeremy, the future of House of Java depends on you," she joked. "On your, um, superior coffee-brewing skills. And as the assistant manager, it's my duty to look after the best interests of the business."

"Oh, is that right?" Jeremy asked, amused.

"Yeah," Jessica said, giggling. "Let's just say . . . if you agree to come back, I'll be sure to think of some way to reward you."

"Uh-oh," Jeremy said. She could picture the adorable, semishocked but pleased expression on his face right now. "I can't turn that down," he said. "I'm just glad I held out for a better contract."

"Great," she said, grinning triumphantly. "Listen, Jeremy, I should probably get back to work. But don't worry—I'll inform the hysterical customers that there's no reason to panic, because Mr. Aames is on his way back."

"Go for it," Jeremy said. "I'll talk to you later."

A shiver shot up Jessica's spine as she hung up the phone. She hadn't been expecting the whole concern-for-Jade routine, but she'd gotten around it okay. Pretty soon Jeremy would be right back where he belonged. He'd be here at HOJ, and more important—he'd be with her.

To: tee@swiftnet.com
cc: marsden1@swiftnet.com
     mslater@swiftnet.com
     evman@swiftnet.com
From: lizw@cal.rr.com

Hey, everyone,
  Can you guys all meet for lunch
tomorrow, off campus at Guido's? It's
<u>urgent</u>. Please be there on time
(Andy), and <u>please</u> make sure you don't
say anything to Conner.
                                        Liz

Big Man on Campus

4

The Great Gatsby. *Biology textbook. Two yellow note-books, three Bic pens, and a mechanical pencil.*

Maria zipped her backpack shut. Yep—she had all her supplies for the next couple of periods. After checking three times, though, it wasn't that big of a surprise.

She sighed, glancing around the crowded hall-way. Where was Ken? He showed up at her locker every single day at this time, right between second and third periods. In fact, she was so used to it that she always felt a rush of excitement at the end of second period.

Maria checked her watch. Only a minute left before the next bell rang. Was he really not going to show? Even after the way he'd treated her on the phone yesterday, going on and on about his coach when she was trying to talk about something that was actually *important*?

She knew he'd probably wanted her to sound happier when he said he had his position back for good, and she did feel guilty about that. But she'd been so scared that—well, *this* would happen. Now that he was big man on campus again, he wouldn't be the same old reliable Ken she depended on.

"Yo, Matthews!" Maria heard a voice rise above the hallway chatter. "Congratulations, man. That was great stuff. . . . I didn't know you still had it in you."

Maria turned in the direction where the voice had come from and finally caught sight of Ken heading toward her. She noticed that all the girls passing by were staring at him like he was a movie star and then giggling with each other as they walked away. Suddenly her boyfriend was the hottest thing in school.

Not that he isn't nice to look at, she reminded herself, softening a little as she took in the way his blue button-down shirt showed off his defined upper body and brought out his incredible eyes.

Just then he saw her, and the warm smile he flashed made it even harder for her to stay annoyed.

"Hey, what's up?" he said as he approached her. "Sorry I'm late—it's crazy; people keep stopping me in the hallway. People I don't even know!" He laughed, shaking his head, and Maria felt a little twist inside but ignored it.

"Just don't let it go to your head," she teased, half serious. She punched him lightly on the shoulder. "Remember who your *real* fans are."

He grinned. "Oh, you mean the college scouts?"

She groaned, right as the bell started ringing.

"We'd better go," she said, reaching up to close her locker. "Hey, don't forget—dinner with my parents tonight."

"Right," he said, nodding. "What time should I get there?"

"Around seven," she said, slinging her bag over her shoulder. She stood there for a second, waiting for him to give her a kiss on the cheek, a hug— something to reassure her that he still wanted to be with *her,* not all those giggly girls.

"Okay, so I'll see you later," he said, jogging off down the hall without even touching her at all.

Yeah. Right. See you later. Maria stood there for a moment, watching everyone rush by her on their way to class.

Snap out of it. She was being way too paranoid, the kind of thing that got her in trouble fast even when there wasn't anything actually wrong. *Especially* when there wasn't anything wrong. With a little shake, she started walking toward her class.

"His name's Ken . . . something. He's the new quarterback," she heard a female voice say as she rounded the corner.

Glancing over, she spotted three freshman girls huddled in a circle outside a classroom, clutching their books in wide-eyed gossip mode.

"Isn't he cute?" another one said, her high pony-tail bouncing as she spoke.

"He's beyond cute," the first girl said. "He's

seriously hot. We *have* to find a way to meet him."

Without thinking, Maria marched over to the trio of girls, pausing for a moment to let her five-foot-eleven frame sufficiently intimidate them. They stared up at her with matching expressions of confusion and nervousness.

"You're right. He *is* hot," she said. "He's also my boyfriend—so leave it alone."

They glanced around at each other, then back at her. "Um, sorry," ponytail girl said quietly. "We didn't know he had a girlfriend."

Now you know, Maria thought. *And you can spread the word to all your little friends.* She whirled around and continued walking down the hall, wishing that had given her the satisfaction she needed. But if being the star quarterback's girlfriend meant constantly looking over your shoulder at the competition, she wasn't sure how long she could handle it.

Elizabeth strode into Guido's pizzeria on Monday afternoon with Andy, Evan, Maria, and Tia right behind her. They'd had a pretty quiet car ride over from SVH since Elizabeth hadn't wanted to get into it until they were here, sitting face-to-face.

"Good afternoon," the host, a guy with slicked-back dark hair, greeted her. "You can sit wherever you like."

"Thanks." Elizabeth paused, surveying the place.

Circular booths with red vinyl seats filled up most of the room, and there was a full row of stools at the front counter. She recognized some SVH students at one of the booths near the front, so she headed straight to the back, sitting down at a table next to the rest rooms.

"Good choice," Andy said, plopping down next to her. "In case of emergency."

Elizabeth let out a sigh as she waited for her friends to get settled. Right now she just wasn't in the mood for Andy's jokes.

"So do we have to wait to order before we hear what this little Yalta summit is about?" Andy asked, brushing a piece of lint off his khaki pants.

"I think we already know," Tia said, leaning forward across the table. Her large brown eyes were filled with concern. "It's about Conner's drinking, right?"

Elizabeth picked up the big plastic menu lying in front of her and started flipping it over in her hands.

"Hey, it's okay," Evan's gentle voice reassured her. She glanced up at him, and he had the same calm, soothing expression he'd had on Saturday morning, when he was telling her about Conner's fall at Crescent Beach. He held her gaze, and she could almost feel herself getting stronger.

"Yeah, you're right," she told Tia. "Mrs. Sandborn came to see me yesterday. She's pretty sure—she thinks Conner could be an alcoholic."

Elizabeth took in all of their faces at once—Andy's raised eyebrows, Maria's stern frown, and Tia and Evan's knowing, worried gazes.

"So what's the next step?" Maria asked.

Elizabeth mustered a small, grateful smile. She'd been through all the emotional turmoil of trying to accept this, and now she just needed to *deal*. It was a relief to have someone like Maria around, someone who was all about taking action.

"I know the guy's looking a little rough around the edges lately," Andy said, scratching his head, "but are you sure it's that serious? Is his mom maybe a little paranoid? You know, because of her own issues."

Evan was looking right at her when she turned to him for help, and he gave her a slight, encouraging nod, then cleared his throat.

"Nobody's being paranoid," he said softly. "Conner's in trouble."

There was a thick, long silence, and Elizabeth stared down at the Formica table, trying to hold back tears. God—hadn't she cried enough the past couple of days? How could there still be more ready to pour out of her?

It was just that sitting here talking about Conner like he was some foreign creature, some specimen they had to diagnose, instead of the guy she was in love with . . . she couldn't stand it for much longer. In fact, she wasn't sure how she'd be getting through this if Evan wasn't there to take over.

"So we're back to my question," Maria finally said. "How can we help?"

Elizabeth licked her lips. She wished the waiter would come over with some water, but he must have noticed they were involved in an intense conversation because he hadn't even taken their order yet. "Conner's mom said we have to do something called an intervention," she said. "I looked it up on the Internet after she left. It's like we all show up at his house and wait for him, then we tell him that we know he's an—that he's sick, but we're all here to support him."

"No way," Tia blurted out. She shook her head hard, her dark ponytail swinging back and forth. "Conner would *freak*."

Elizabeth flinched. That was exactly what she'd been afraid of. And if Tia agreed with her . . . As much as she didn't like to admit it, Tia really did know Conner at least as well as she did. Maybe better.

But Mrs. Sandborn knows what she's talking about, Elizabeth reminded herself. "You're right," she said. "He's not going to take it well—but it's the only option. I just need to know if you guys are in." She looked around at each of them.

"Yeah, of course," Andy piped up. "I'll be there. But do you think this actually has a shot of working?"

If this *didn't* work, Elizabeth thought, then her

53

boyfriend would be in so deep, she wasn't sure what could save him.

"I think we have a chance," Evan answered in her place. "Tia? Maria? You up for it? Things could get ugly, you know."

Tia clasped her hands on the table. "If you really think it's right," she began, glancing back and forth between Evan and Elizabeth, "then I'll be there."

"Thanks, Tee," Elizabeth said, feeling a rush of gratitude. She knew it was a big step for Tia to trust her on something this huge. They were risking a lot.

"You know you can count on me," Maria promised. She reached out and put her hand over Elizabeth's.

"Okay, so we should all start thinking about what to say," Elizabeth said, giving Maria another half smile. She gazed around the room, looking for the waiter so they could finally place their order. "Because if we're doing this, it has to be soon."

Otherwise I'll probably lose my nerve, she added silently.

Ken faked a pass, dodged the outstretched arms of the opposing linebacker, then sliced and diced down the field, riding a wave of blocks for a full twenty yards before the whistle finally blew.

"Great stuff, Matthews!" Coach Riley yelled. "If you can rush like that in the game, we might not even need to run any pass plays."

Ken felt the pride surge through him as he jogged back to the huddle. He was in "the zone" this practice—that place where every move he made on the field was the right one. He wasn't even thinking at all, just *acting* from natural instinct. Perfect passes on the run, faking out defenders, running like the wind down the sidelines . . . he couldn't even believe what he was accomplishing.

As he got closer to his teammates, he slowed to a walk, wiping the sweat off his face. "All right," he said, latching his arms over the broad shoulders of Todd Wilkins and Matt Wells to join the huddle. Hot, moist breath hit his face from both sides, and a dozen helmeted faces were focused on him. "This is the last play, so we're going for it. Run the same option, but this time I'll fake a handoff to Wells . . . then throw long to Wilkins. Got it? Break!"

"Break!"

The whole team filed into position in seconds, and Ken cleared his throat. "Twenty-four! Thirty-nine! Hut! Hut! *Hike!*" he called.

He shuffled backward, pivoted, and faked the handoff. Then he veered back and to his left, stopping to look downfield for Wilkins. He was totally covered. Ken heard the loud grunt of an oncoming defensive lineman just a few feet to his left, arms outstretched like a wild animal. He lunged forward, feeling a hand slap against his thigh. *Come on, Todd.*

"Release the ball!" Coach shouted from the sidelines.

Not yet, he thought. *We're going for it all.* He heard cleats pounding the ground behind him and ducked off to his right. Looking up again, he saw Todd pulling away into open field about forty yards away. *Now.* Ken took one strong step forward and launched a spiraling rocket pass like a guided missile . . . and *crunch!* He got hammered from the side.

His shoulder rammed hard into the ground, then a heavy load pressed his face into the dirt. Through the corners of his eyes Ken saw a little patch of grass reaching up for his face.

"Yeah!" he heard someone yell.

"Nice pass!"

"Great catch, Wilkins!"

Ken wiggled his way free from his tackler and looked down the field. Todd was jogging back toward him, ball raised over his head. Ken stood up and glanced over at the sideline. They were all cheering, clapping, raising their helmets above their heads. *Wow, this feels good. . . . It's been such a long time.*

Coach Riley blew the whistle. "Perfect!" He shook his fist at Ken and smiled. "You shouldn't ignore your coach," he added, "but it's not always a bad thing to trust your instincts either. Offense, you can hit the showers. Defense, you take a lap around the track."

Ken pulled off his helmet and started heading

toward the locker room. The late afternoon sun shone on his sweaty face, his arms felt light, and there was a confident rhythm in his stride that he hadn't felt in a while. He looked over at the guys on the sideline, considering jogging toward them for more showers of congratulations. But it wasn't his style to soak it up like that, and right now his team needed to feel like he was pulling them together—not trying to ride over them.

Besides, maybe today's a freak thing, he thought. Well, today *and* the game Saturday. A line from his dad's article in the *Tribune* ran through his mind. *"Matthews shook the rust off after one play and with his strong arm carried SVH to yet another solid victory."*

"Yo, Matthews!"

Ken turned around and saw Todd Wilkins jogging toward him.

"Great practice," Todd said when he reached him. They fell into step together, walking toward the locker room side by side. "Listen, we're all gonna go see Will at the hospital now. I figured you'd want to come with us. . . ."

Ken stopped at the door to the locker room. He ran his hand over his sweat-drenched, short blond hair, trying to figure out what to say. Visiting Will was the last thing he felt like doing. He'd never really known the guy, and now he was benefiting from his injury.

"I don't know," Ken said. He pushed open the locker door and stepped inside. "You sure he'd want to see me?"

"Oh, yeah," Todd said, nodding. "He's got it pretty rough, but he still wants the team to stay on top of things, and you're the man now." Todd paused, glancing around at the other players changing around them. He leaned his head in toward Ken, lowering his voice. "And I think the rest of the guys would feel better knowing there's no hard feelings," he said.

Ken sighed, sinking down on the bench in the middle of the locker room. Todd was right—it would look pretty bad not to show up if most of the team was going. He couldn't refuse to visit the injured quarterback whose position he'd taken. But he kept feeling like there was something he was supposed to do, somewhere else he had to go. . . .

It can't be more important than this. He had to show his team spirit, and now was a good time to start.

"Yeah, sure," Ken said. "I'll go."

"Cool," Todd said, hitting Ken on the shoulder pads. "Meet me at my locker after you shower up, okay?" He turned and walked away without waiting for an answer.

"Uh-huh," Ken muttered to Todd's back. Even though everything Todd had said made sense, he couldn't help feeling like going to visit Will would be a big mistake.

Maria Slater

I'm not sure why, but for some reason I did this major closet excavation when I got home from school today. Maybe all this stuff with Ken and Liz and Conner just made me want to regress or something.

Anyway, I found all my old diaries, pictures, Valentine's Day cards, and this Wonder Woman lunch box that I used to carry every single day. I even found a note from Ezra Edelman that he gave me in fifth grade, asking, "Will you go with me? Circle Yes, No, or Maybe." None of them were circled . . . but I think I ended up telling him yes, and then we "went out" for about three days before deciding to "just be friends."

It was fun until I saw my old Barbie dolls. I was never too into Barbie, but some relative gave me a few of them once for my birthday.

She also gave me a Ken doll. He's wearing a

varsity letter jacket—and with the blond hair, square jaw, and blue eyes, he looks kind of like . . . my Ken. My boyfriend, Ken.

I know I'm being totally crazy. But right as I went to put away the Ken doll, I spotted Cheerleader Barbie. Plastic smile, too much makeup, one pom-pom raised, yellow blond hair . . . the complete opposite of me. And she's supposed to be Ken's ideal mate, right?

I mean, the Ken doll's ideal mate.

Andy Marsden

<u>Reasons to Avoid the Intervention</u>

1. He'll definitely walk out, and he won't talk to any of us for at least a decade.
2. I don't think I could say a cheesy line like, "We're only here because we care about you," with a straight face.
3. Don't I have enough to deal with right now?

<u>Reasons to Show Up for the Intervention</u>

1. It's Conner.

CHAPTER
Roadblocks
5

Jade pulled into the Big Mesa parking lot, pausing at the entrance to check her watch. 5:13. Perfect. Jeremy would be getting out of practice any second.

She gently pressed down on the accelerator, coasting through the lot as she searched for the perfect spot. She wanted to be close enough to see the parade of players walking from the field toward the locker room but far enough not to be *obvious.*

Finally choosing a space about a hundred yards from the field, she parked the car and turned off the engine, then immediately yanked down the rearview mirror to do a face inspection.

I could use a little touch-up, she decided. She had come straight to Big Mesa after cheerleading practice, without taking any prep time after her quick shower. *Nothing some lipstick can't help.* She fished through her backpack and pulled out her favorite shade, a nice, deep cinnamon color that contrasted well with her olive skin.

After applying a couple of coats, Jade tossed it back in her bag and glanced over at the field, sitting up straighter as she glimpsed a few broad guys in sweats and football jerseys trudging across the grass.

Time to move. With a little flip of her hair to increase the body, she got out of her car and slammed the door behind her. A steady stream of sweaty guys were passing by now, and one of them called out to her as she approached. She gave him a friendly wave but immediately returned her focus to the others, searching for Jeremy.

Finally she saw him, walking by himself with his helmet swinging from his right hand. She drew a deep breath and pasted a calm, hopefully radiant smile on her face. "Jeremy," she said, loud enough to grab his attention but not so loud that she'd seem desperate.

He stopped, then swung his gaze in her direction. His eyebrows shot up when he saw her. "Jade?"

She paused, watching his expression closely. All she could really make out was confusion and surprise. At least his warm brown eyes weren't filling with rage the way they had Friday night, when he'd caught her kissing Josh.

"Hey," she responded, widening her smile. She took a few steps closer, and his legs apparently came unstuck because he jogged across the remaining distance between them.

"I was just, you know, thinking about you," Jade said once they stood face-to-face. "So I thought I'd come by and say hi." She'd never seen him out of his casual-prep look before. His upper body looked *nice* in the thin T-shirt clinging to his skin under his jersey.

Jeremy scratched his head with his free hand, brushing a few strands of dark hair away from his eyes. "I heard about what happened at House of Java," he said. "Sorry about that—it must really suck."

Jade struggled not to reveal her surprise. She'd been prepared for another tongue-lashing like the one she'd gotten at Crescent Beach. But he was already feeling bad for her—this was going to be much easier than she'd expected.

It would have been the perfect time to slip in the info that Jessica had probably left out—the part where *she* was the one who got Jade fired. But Jade knew that guys hated that kind of catty, immature stuff. It was better to wait and let him find out the truth himself.

Jade shrugged. "Things just weren't working there," she said. "It happens."

Jeremy nodded, then kicked at some rocks on the ground, staring out at the parking lot behind her.

He's waiting for me to get to the point—to say why I'm really here. Well, this was definitely a good time.

She stepped closer to him, fixing him with her most sincere, apologetic gaze. "I'm the one who needs to say I'm sorry here anyway," she began. She rubbed her palms along the sides of her tight black jeans, trying to achieve the perfect combination of nervousness and guilty regret. "About the other night . . . I should have told you I was seeing Josh."

She stopped, observing the slight clenching of his jaw. He was fighting emotion. *Yes.*

"I *wanted* to tell you," she continued, letting her bottom lip quiver just slightly. "But I knew I was breaking up with him, and I didn't want to mess everything up with us for nothing. I was going to end it that night, I swear. But then you and Jessica showed up, and things got out of control."

Jeremy's eyes softened as he looked down at her, and she could definitely recognize hope mixed in with all the hurt. He wanted to believe her—he just had to let himself. So maybe her version of the truth was a little twisted, but it wasn't a lie that she wanted Jeremy and that Josh was history. That was all that mattered, right?

On a hunch she decided to lighten the mood. She clasped her hands in front of her face. "Can you *ever* forgive me?" she teased in as melodramatic a voice as possible.

She'd almost forgotten how adorable his smile was—but the faint one that crossed his lips now was enough to make her heart beat just a little faster.

"I promise I'll make everything up to you," she added, sensing her advantage growing. "I'll, um, take you to dinner—whatever you want." She stared up at him with her best inviting expression, hoping he'd get the message.

He squinted at her. "Okay," he said, tilting his head to the side. "But we're not going out."

Jade's eyes widened. "Oh, really?" This was much better than she'd expected.

"No—we're staying in." He stretched his arms out over his head, giving her a glimpse of his perfectly toned stomach. "My house, tomorrow night. Seven okay?"

"Definitely," she agreed, trying to contain her excitement. *Never lose your cool. Not when you have things just the way you want them.* She'd hit a small roadblock, but she was clearly back on track.

There's only one way to defeat Gene the Germ, kids! You guessed it—Sammy Soap! Nothing kills germs like Sammy Soap—

Ken shut the pamphlet and tossed it across the table, staring down at the cover in disgust. A big, red blob shape with googly eyes smiled at him above the title, "Bacteria Wars!"

He had been waiting so long in the Fowler Memorial Hospital waiting room that he'd already been through all the decent reading materials. Two issues of *Sports Illustrated,* one *Entertainment Weekly*—Ken had even checked out *Better Homes and Gardens* before moving on to the educational pamphlets.

He glanced over at his teammates. They were sitting around the table a few feet away, engrossed in a conversation about football. He knew he should be joining in, but he just wasn't in the mood. He was so anxious about seeing Will, and the nurses kept making them wait while the doctors went in and out of his room. Meanwhile on the drive over here he'd remembered what he was supposed to do tonight—dinner with Maria and her parents.

It was just after six-thirty now, so if they got in to see Will in the next couple of minutes, he'd only be a little late for dinner. He'd been putting off calling her unless he had to because he'd been hoping he could still make it on time and he didn't want to get her all upset.

Besides, what am I supposed to tell her? It really *didn't* make sense for him to be here. What could he possibly say to Will that would make him feel better? If Ken was the one lying in that bed, wondering if he'd ever play again . . . he wouldn't want to talk to anyone for weeks. Okay, maybe Maria. But he definitely wouldn't be psyched to see the guy who'd taken his position. This was such a waste of . . .

"Okay, everyone, you can see Will now."

Ken looked up and recognized the petite, red-haired young nurse who'd been giving them updates every couple of minutes. She smiled at them. "I'm sure he'll be so happy to see all of you," she said.

I don't know about that, Ken thought. He stood, straightening his pants, then trailed the other guys as they followed the nurse through the gray waiting-room doors and down the hall. The scent of medicine and sterile alcohol was overwhelming, and the people being wheeled by with IVs coming out of their arms was starting to freak him out. He'd never really been around sick people.

The nurse stepped into a room almost at the end of the hallway, then turned to beckon them in after her.

"Hi, Will," she announced cheerfully as she pulled aside the curtain that surrounded his bed. "Your friends are here to visit. I'm going to leave you with them, but I'll be back to check on you soon."

On her way out of the room she stopped next to Ken. "He might be a little groggy from the medications," she said, keeping her voice down. "But try to keep him positive."

Ken nodded, wondering why she'd chosen him to give the information to. How could it not be obvious that he was the last person who deserved that responsibility?

"Simmons," Matt said once the nurse had left. He moved forward awkwardly. "How are you, man?"

"I'm okay," Will replied. Ken couldn't actually see him over the heads of his teammates, but he recognized the voice.

"Hey, you should go say something," Todd said, giving Ken a nudge with his elbow. "Tell him you won't let the team down."

Ken swallowed hard, wishing he'd never agreed to come here. Then he edged forward, squeezing between Josh Radinsky and Brian Cogley.

He opened his mouth to say something along the lines of what Todd had suggested, but as soon as he saw Will, his jaw just hung open, no words coming out. It was . . . horrible.

Will was lying there with tubes coming out of him and his entire leg in a giant cast, suspended in the air with some big contraption. His face was freakishly pale and his lips all dry and cracked. Ken had never seen anything like it. Someone who just days ago was on top of his form now looking so *weak* and helpless.

"Um . . . hey," he finally got out.

Will's eyes hardened, and Ken was sure he glimpsed pure hatred, so strong, it made him suck in his breath. Then Will turned his head to face the wall. "You should go," he said, his voice flat. "All of you. I want to be alone."

Guilt ripped through Ken. He should have trusted his gut and stayed away from here. Seeing him—the new star quarterback—healthy and walking around was the last thing the guy needed. And now he wouldn't even let his friends stick around.

"I'm sorry," he muttered, then whirled around and

pushed his way out of the room, letting his teammates decide for themselves whether to stay or go.

Where is he? Maria gritted her teeth as she stared down at the steaming plate of food her mother had just placed in front of her. Roast chicken breast, thick mashed potatoes, and a huge salad. It smelled so good, she wanted to dig right in, but they were still waiting for Ken, hoping he was only running a few minutes late and would ring the doorbell any second.

"I'm sure he'll be here," Maria's mom assured her as she sat down in her seat across the table. Maria looked up at her, barely containing a sigh. Her parents had just started to actually *care* about her life, and Ken knew what a big deal it was to her for him to get to know them a little better. How could he ditch her like this? She looked over at her dad, sitting at the head of the long, oval table. He was clearly impatient—he had that little annoyed crease in his forehead, with the matching tight-lipped frown.

"We might as well start without him," Maria said. "Who knows when he'll show up." She jammed her fork into the mashed potatoes, scooping up a large mouthful. The smooth, buttery taste was satisfying but not enough to calm her down. Instead of taking another bite she dragged her fork along the white mush, making lines across the potatoes as she tried to picture what Ken was doing right now. Practicing late. Showing Coach Riley how committed he was to the team by running extra sprints. Or maybe he was in the locker room, talking to the guys about football and breasts and Jennifer Love Hewitt . . . whatever guys talked about.

But it's already after seven. Even if he practiced late, Ken should be out of the locker room by now. The indentations in the mashed potatoes got deeper as she continued to pull her fork back and forth.

"I'm really surprised," Mr. Slater said, pausing between bites of chicken. "Ken seems very nice. I'm sure there was just some kind of miscommunication."

"Yeah," Maria agreed, even though she knew he'd heard her reminder about dinner loud and clear this morning. "You're probably right."

The phone rang, and Maria jumped, bumping her knees against the table. "Excuse me," she said. "Maybe that's him." She pushed back her chair and practically ran into the other room to grab the phone before the answering machine picked up.

"Hello?" she answered, breathless.

"Maria, hey. I'm *so* sorry."

Ken. He sounded tired, but not upset—not panicky like there'd been an emergency.

"What happened?" she demanded, keeping her voice low so her parents couldn't hear from the dining room.

"It's kind of a long story," he replied.

"I'll take the short version," she said, tapping the floor with her shoe. He wasn't getting off the hook

72

that easily, not with her parents sitting in the other room thinking her boyfriend had just stood her—and them—up.

He sighed. "After practice Todd asked me to come with him and the other guys to visit Will at the hospital," he said. "I figured we'd be done in time for me to make it to dinner, but it took a while to get in his room." He paused, and when he continued, his voice sounded strained. "Then the second Will saw me, he pretty much freaked. He told us all to leave. I don't know what they did, but I got out fast. I felt really bad. So . . . I guess I just wasn't up for dinner after that. Not tonight. I'm really sorry, Maria. We can do this another night, though, right?"

"Yeah, sure," she said. It did sound like he'd had a rough afternoon—and he'd only been trying to do the right thing. At least he wasn't just goofing around with the guys. But still, shouldn't she have been more of a priority? "You could have called earlier," she muttered.

"I kept thinking we would see Will any second," he explained. "Then after I saw him, I just wanted to get home, you know?"

"Okay," she said. "I guess I understand. I'll figure out something to tell my parents."

"Thanks," he said, obviously relieved. "And I really will make this up to you."

"Yeah," she teased. "You will." She just wished she wasn't having such a tough time believing that.

Elizabeth Wakefield

<u>Abigail Swift</u>

Abigail and Lionel had been best
friends since before they learned to
fly. Lionel's nest was only a couple of
branches away, and they played
together daily.

"Can Lionel come out to play?" she'd
quail, and then it was all hopping around,
throwing seeds at each other, and
making forts out of twigs.

When Abigail and Lionel first spread
their wings for takeoff, their mothers
let them fly together. They hopped
off The Tree, the only place they'd
known, and sailed past forests and
cliffs, over the gyrating ocean. When

they finally landed, it was on an electric wire overlooking a busy street. Abigail wasn't pleased with the concrete and cars, she didn't know how to get home, and she worried about the look on Lionel's face.

"I like it here," he cooed.

Abigail didn't say a word.

From that day on, Lionel thought of only one thing: flying adventures. At first Lionel was content with speed—swifts _were_ the fastest animals in the whole world anyway—and Abigail could handle that. But that wasn't enough for Lionel. He needed danger. He flew way too close to the water—at that speed, hitting the water would be instant death. Lionel also forced Abigail to follow him into the city, where he'd met a threesome of dirty, shady pigeons. It was with these pigeons, named Ricky and Donnie and Joey, that Lionel tried bird nip for the first time. He was in such a stupor from it that Abigail had to carry him home on her back.

That night Abigail couldn't sleep. She kept thinking about Lionel, about his dangerous air dives and the dazed look in his bird-nipped eyes. What had happened to Lionel? Abigail missed him. Even worse, she feared he might not be around much longer.

The next day Abigail didn't go to Lionel's nest, so he eventually came over to hers. "Ready to go?" he asked. Abigail shook her head no. She stuttered away about how Lionel was playing with fire, how she hated his new pigeon friends, how she couldn't stand the thought of him bursting into feathery flames because he flew too close to the water.

Lionel just looked at her. Then he flew away.

Abigail didn't see Lionel for an entire year—a long time in bird years—and during that year she cried a lot. She made new friends, but nothing could replace the empty spot she had for Lionel.

One day Abigail heard a screechy groan outside her nest. She hopped outside and saw a bird in the distance, dangling on a rocky precipice, feathers reddened by blood. It was Lionel. Without hesitation Abigail swooped down, grabbed Lionel, and brought him back to her nest. She nursed him for the entire day, tending to his wounds and feeding him worm soup. And they talked. Lionel described his many adventures, Abigail talked about her new friends—it was as if nothing had ever changed.

And from that day on, nothing did change. Because Lionel and Abigail fell in love, and they never again fell out—of love, or of that nest, which they stayed in together for the rest of their lives. Lionel maintained his appetite for adventure, but he promised Abigail he'd be careful. . . . Besides, he couldn't wait to teach Lionel Jr. how to fly.

CHAPTER 6
Officially Irrelevant

I never realized Sweet Valley High's hallways were so deserted this early, Ken thought as he walked down the hall on Tuesday morning. Without the noise of kids talking and lockers opening and slamming around him, he could even hear the soft sound of his sneakers hitting the floor. He had woken up a full hour before his alarm was set to go off this morning, and he hadn't been able to get back to sleep. So here he was, in school a good half hour before the first bell.

He was thinking how nice it was to have the place to himself when he rounded the corner and saw someone standing in front of a locker, just staring inside without moving.

The figure seemed familiar. . . . But he couldn't place her. He kept moving closer, and she didn't turn around, but finally it hit him with a jolt.

Melissa Fox—Will's girlfriend. He stopped, watching her uneasily. She looked so *little* in her loose jeans and sweatshirt, her long, brown hair falling almost halfway down her slender back.

But what's she doing? he wondered. It was like she was frozen in place.

With a deep breath Ken quickly started striding toward her. He wasn't sure why, but he felt this weird responsibility to make sure she was okay. None of this was his fault—but that didn't seem to make a difference.

"Hey, Melissa," he said. Without even thinking, he reached out and laid his hand on her small shoulder.

She shrank from his hand and whirled around, her expression morphing from shock to anger when she saw it was him. "What do you think you're doing?" she spat out. "First you show up at the hospital to see Will, and now you're—you're *touching* me?"

Ken took a few steps back from her, stuffing his hands in his pockets. "I just—I wanted to make sure you were okay," he mumbled.

She snorted. "Right," she said. "I'm sure you feel *terrible* about being the star quarterback again, scoring the winning touchdown in the game Saturday. Please." She slammed her locker door shut, and he noticed that her hands were trembling slightly. Her tone was confident, but something was off. . . . He had a feeling she wasn't as in control as she was acting.

Still, it didn't give her the right to say that stuff to him. "Look," he said, shrugging his backpack higher on his shoulder. "I really am sorry about what happened to Will, whether or not you believe it. But it's not my fault he got hurt." Yeah, maybe a small part of him had hoped that Will would bump his leg a little, just enough to force him to sit out for a couple of plays. But he'd *never* wanted Will to be injured this badly—and even if he had, he wasn't responsible for it actually happening.

"Just do me a favor, okay?" Melissa asked, focusing her striking blue eyes on his face. He squinted, trying to see if those were tears or just the light hitting her a certain way. "Stay away from Will. Because maybe if you'd never shown up there in the first place—" She stopped, and the pain in her expression was so intense that Ken couldn't help feeling a rush of sympathy. But before he could say anything, she spun around and flew off down the hallway.

Ken stood there watching her until she'd disappeared around the corner. He'd always thought Melissa Fox wasn't capable of feeling anything beyond contempt for anyone she considered below her—which was pretty much everybody. But he'd glimpsed something *real* in her eyes just then. Whatever she'd cut herself off from saying was major, and it was killing her.

And for some reason, he needed to know what it was.

Conner made his way through the packed SVH hallway, glaring at everyone around him. *This place is full of bad vibes.* Glancing to his left, he saw the inside of some girl's locker door, covered in magazine pictures of the latest hot boy band. *These people are all so pointless,* he thought, shaking his head.

He still had the remnants of yesterday's headache, and his stomach felt a little uneasy. He was starting to wonder if he was coming down with the flu. It wasn't like he'd had that much to drink last night. He reached up to rub his head, briefly shutting his eyes.

Suddenly he felt the impact of another person crash into him. He stepped backward, then looked down to see who he'd walked into. He blinked.

Elizabeth. Of course.

She stared up at him, her blue-green eyes hesitant and . . . scared. God. She was afraid of him. She was also beautiful—in an instant he'd absorbed the way the soft, dipping neckline of her navy cotton shirt showed off her perfect skin. He also noticed the few strands of light blond hair that had slipped out of her loose ponytail, framing her face.

His heart rate sped up, as if he were a character in some stupid romance novel. He hated the way Elizabeth had this effect on him, no matter how many times he'd been around her.

"Hey—do you want to talk?" Elizabeth asked softly.

Conner forced his eyes away from her, focusing on the floor instead. He felt a thin layer of sweat form on the back of his neck. Did he want to talk?

No. What he wanted was to grab her and hold her so tightly that he could smell the faint, flowery smell of her shampoo. He wanted to kiss her, to lose himself in the sensation of her lips pressed against his. . . .

"Conner?" Her voice sounded far away, like she was calling to him across some big expanse. And she might as well have been. He shook himself, chasing the silly fantasy out of his brain. If kissing Elizabeth was as simple as that, then no problem. But it wasn't—because after the kiss there would be questions, and pressures that he couldn't handle.

Without a word, Conner shoved right past Elizabeth and continued down the hallway. He thought he heard her let out a small sigh as he passed her, but he wasn't going to stop. He wasn't going to care.

Because Elizabeth, like just about everyone else at Sweet Valley High, was now officially *irrelevant*.

"So then he said I should just forget about it, but I don't think he's right because—" Maria stopped, realizing that Andy wasn't hearing a word she'd said. They were walking up to the cafeteria together, and Maria was filling Andy in on the latest with Ken. At least, she'd *thought* she was until she noticed that he was a million miles away. She felt a stab of guilt—Andy must have a lot of stuff on his mind too. It had only been a little while since he'd told all of them that he was gay. He just seemed so cool about it, it was hard to remember that maybe he *wasn't*.

"Andy," she said, raising her voice to break him out of his thoughts. They started heading up the stairs to the second floor, sticking to the side to avoid the crowd squeezing by them. "Are you okay?"

Andy's head jerked a little in surprise. "Huh? Why?" he asked, narrowly avoiding a collision with some freshman who came zooming down the stairs.

"You just seem a little distracted," she said carefully, moving closer to him. "If you want to talk about anything . . ."

He flashed her a smile. "Thanks," he said. "I guess with all this Conner stuff, everyone's kind of forgotten about—well, you know, what I said."

She nodded. "Have you told Conner?" she asked.

"Yeah, actually, I did." He shrugged. "I don't think it really mattered to him, with all the other things he's going through right now. But at least he didn't freak. You know, he wasn't even *surprised*."

Maria held back a smile. None of them had been shocked by his news. Yeah, it was a big deal to hear it and everything—but once she'd thought about it, it made sense. Back when Andy was going out with Six, something had seemed . . . not right. Now she knew why.

They reached the top of the stairs and joined the throng of people moving toward the cafeteria.

"I guess if Liz and everyone is right about him, then he sort of has an excuse for the way he acted," Andy went on. "What really bugs me is people like

Tia. How many hours have I spent listening to her talk about her problems? But now that it's me dealing with something, no one's around."

"Wow, Andy—I'm sorry," Maria said. She'd had no idea he felt that way. "I'm sure if you said something to her or to Liz, they'd be there for you."

"Yeah, aren't girls supposed to be the less self-absorbed gender?" he said sarcastically.

"Maybe they're just not as totally self-*consumed*," Maria said, her thoughts returning to Ken. "But it also depends on the person," she couldn't help adding. "Like, Ken used to be one of the least self-centered people I know. Now suddenly he's star quarterback again, and it's like no one else even exists."

Before Andy could respond, a loud voice from behind them bellowed, "Man, it's gonna be awesome!"

Maria and Andy half turned, and Maria saw a couple of guys she recognized from the football team. "Hey, you're Matthews's girlfriend, right?" one of the guys asked when he caught her looking at him. She couldn't remember his name, but she'd seen him a few times when she'd met up with Ken right after practice. The guy was huge, with dark, thick hair, big eyes, and scraggly facial hair.

Maria nodded reluctantly, perfectly content to avoid any interaction with the oaf.

"So, are you pumped for tomorrow night?" he asked.

Tomorrow night? She bit her lip, wondering what

he meant. An uneasy feeling came over her. If this guy was psyched for it, then she probably wouldn't be, whatever it was.

"Come on!" the other guy piped up. He was shorter and stockier than the first one but seemed just as annoying. "The huge football bash in honor of your man! You're going, right?"

Maria gulped, glancing quickly at Andy. A deep blush spread over her cheeks. How completely mortifying—these random guys knew more about her boyfriend's plans for the week than *she* did. How could Ken not tell her about this? Was he just going to go without her?

"Yeah," the bushy-haired one chimed in, apparently not noticing Maria's embarrassment. "Your boyfriend is the guest of honor, the star attraction. He's, like, the reason we're having the party."

They were throwing a party *in honor of Ken*— and he'd forgotten to mention that?

"You better be ready to drive your guy home," stocky guy added. They both started laughing in that irritating, guffaw kind of way. "Because he's gonna get hazed out of his mind."

Ha ha ha. Maria looked at Andy again, hoping he'd help her out of this before she went ballistic on these guys. Since when did Ken get wasted like that—*especially* on a school night? Maria's hands clenched into fists at her sides.

"You think I can come to this bash, guys?" Andy

said, giving Maria a reassuring glance. "I'd love to, you know, check out the raw brainpower in the room. I bet the conversation will be *riveting*."

The two of them stared at Andy with identical expressions of confusion and annoyance. If Maria weren't there, he would probably get his head smashed for that one.

"Thanks, guys," Maria said, hooking her arm through Andy's. "We'd better get going." She dragged Andy along with her down the hall, away from the ticked-off football players.

First Ken skipped dinner with her parents, and now he was going to some football party without even telling her about it? It was time for a serious conversation with the new it guy.

To: mfox@starnet.com
From: kenQB@swiftnet.com
Re: This morning

Melissa—
    I did a Web search, and I think
this is Melissa Fox from Sweet Valley
High. If it's you, I just wanted to
let you know that I feel really bad
about what happened today. I'll be at
your locker after last period if you
want to talk.

To: kenQB@swiftnet.com
From: mfox@starnet.com

Dear Ken—
   Um, I do go to Sweet Valley High,
but my name's Melanie. By the way,
are you Ken QB, like, the football-
team-quarterback Ken?
   WB

                    Mel

CHAPTER 7

Solo Celebration

Where is she? Ken sighed, leaning against Melissa's locker. He had to leave for practice soon. Now wasn't the best time to show up late. But he really wanted to see Melissa first and make sure she was okay, especially after the discovery that his e-mail had gone to the completely wrong person.

He knew it was crazy to be here anyway. Melissa had pretty much told him that the last person on earth she wanted to be around was him. But that vulnerable glint in her eyes before she'd run away . . . as if she'd actually *wanted* to tell him something that she was holding inside. He knew that what happened to her and her boyfriend was not his fault, but he couldn't stop feeling responsible.

Which is why I'm here, he told himself, ignoring the small voice inside him that said maybe there was something more.

Ken glanced at his watch again, shifting his weight. If she didn't turn up in the next forty-five seconds, then—

"What are you doing here?" The cold, high-pitched voice sent a strange chill down his spine.

He turned around, and Melissa stood in front of him, staring up at him with those same large, impossibly piercing blue eyes.

Obviously she hadn't gotten the e-mail. Ken racked his brain for the apology he'd rehearsed, but the words weren't there.

"I, um, I wanted to say I'm sorry again. For visiting Will and for—whatever else," he said lamely. He tugged at the bottom of his button-down shirt, feeling the need to keep his hands busy. "So, are you . . . okay?"

"Fine," Melissa snapped. "Everything's fine. Don't worry—you've done your good-guy act, okay? So you're free to leave." She waved her hand in the air to emphasize the statement, and her voice was just as solid as it had been earlier. But he could sense that same panic in her expression, like she was right on the verge of losing it big time.

Ignoring her words, Ken took a step closer to Melissa, his eyes locked on hers. The intensity of her gaze gave him a weird feeling in his stomach. "Listen, if there's something else, um, something you want to say—" He stopped, worried that he'd mess this up and she'd bolt again. "I can, you know, listen."

Her face remained set in an unwelcoming frown, but he could see her muscles twitch, as if she were still holding back her emotions. "Why should I tell you anything?" she demanded. "I don't even *know* you."

He threw up his arms. "Look, I'm sorry," he repeated for what seemed like the millionth time. "I was just trying to help. But if you really want me to leave you alone, then I'm gone."

He turned to walk away, but he'd only made it one step when she called out to him, softly this time. "Wait," she said.

Slowly he pivoted to face her. The crowd around them had thinned, with most people already gone for the day or off at activity meetings and sports practices. He knew he was going to get a lot of crap from Coach Riley for being late, but right now he couldn't care less.

"I saw Will at the hospital a little while after you left," Melissa admitted. "He made me leave. He said I can't come back—I can't visit him anymore. He—he doesn't want to see me."

Before Ken could respond, she started to cry, the tears rushing each other down her face. He watched as she crumpled back against her locker for support.

Without hesitation Ken stepped forward and wrapped his arms around her tiny frame, letting her fall into him. She threw her arms around his neck, clasping him more tightly to her. Gently he began to rub her back, trying to calm her down.

Finally her sobs slowed to drawn-out sighs, and he began to be acutely aware of how close they were. The feeling of a body other than Maria's long, toned one pressed against him was strange. They were just hugging—but somehow this felt very wrong.

"I'm sure Will didn't mean it," Ken blurted out. He let go of her, pulling back. "He's upset, but he needs you. And he'll realize that soon."

She sniffled, wiping away the tears from her face, then turned to face her locker, probably embarrassed for having fallen apart like that in front of him. He was pretty sure not too many people had seen Melissa Fox cry.

"I mean it," Ken said. He stared at the gentle curve of her neck and shoulders, another twinge of guilt passing through him at the physical response it stirred inside him. "He wouldn't risk losing you," he added quietly.

She looked back at him, her eyes locked on his as if his faith could pass through to her.

"Um, I really have to go," he said. "Practice, you know." She winced, and he realized what an idiot he was to bring that up. "If you—if you need anyone to talk to later . . ." He stopped, suddenly feeling awkward.

He barely knew this girl, and a second ago they were holding each other. What was he doing?

"See you around," he mumbled, then took off down the hall, rushing to the locker room to change. Coach would ride him hard today for being late—

but an intense workout was exactly what he needed right now.

Maria ran down the SVH hallway at top speed, her long legs hurling her forward. She could barely see through the tears clouding her eyes, but she knew she needed to get out of the building as soon as possible, and her body was automatically taking her around the familiar turns to the exit. Her chest burned as she ran, but the pain helped—it pushed her to keep going.

Melissa Fox, she thought, feeling fresh tears gather behind her eyelids. Was that why Ken hadn't told her about the party? He was planning on inviting someone else?

It was crazy, she knew, but so was the idea of her boyfriend holding Melissa so close, they were practically melded together—and she'd just seen that with her own eyes.

She stopped, trying to catch her breath. Normally she knew how to pace herself better, but her emotions were too out of control. This was all happening so fast, like a nightmare or a sick joke. Just days ago everything between her and Ken was *fine*—great, in fact. But now it was just one thing after another. She'd been searching for Ken to ask him about that stupid jock party, and then she'd found him so wrapped up—literally—with Will Simmons's girlfriend that he hadn't even noticed she was standing there.

I should have said something, she told herself, starting down the hall again at a more reasonable speed. But her first instinct had been to bolt. It was like this horrible instant replay of that moment when she'd stood outside Conner's house, looking through his kitchen window as he and Elizabeth kissed.

The memory still sent a jab of hurt through her, even though she'd been over Conner for aeons now. It was one thing not to care about the guy anymore, but she wasn't sure she'd ever get over the way it felt to be betrayed like that. And Ken knew what she'd been through with Conner and Elizabeth—so how could he do it to her all over again?

Suddenly she lost her balance, and before she could think, she was on the floor, hitting the cold linoleum at an awkward angle with the right side of her body. She felt the ache everywhere—her ribs, her leg, the palm of her hand. She sat there for a moment, her backpack lying next to her, feeling utterly pathetic.

This is ridiculous. With a deep breath she stood up, rubbing her side. She was *not* going to let herself flip out like this. She was going to calm down and deal. Maybe he'd have a perfectly good explanation—for the party, for Melissa, for everything he'd been doing the past couple of days.

And if not? she asked herself as she started to walk down the hall again. *If not, then forget him,* she thought. If Ken really was doing something with Melissa behind her back, then he wasn't worth it anyway.

Conner sat on the edge of his bed, his eyes half closed as he listened to the mellow blues song coming from his stereo. Even with the light off, the room was still brighter than he would have liked, with the afternoon sun peeking through his drawn shades. He held his guitar in his lap, even though he still couldn't really play with the scrapes all over his hands from his stupid fall on Friday. He tried anyway to trace some chords, ignoring the pain in his fingertips. But the notes were flat, uninspired. He tossed the guitar onto his bed behind him and fell back against the mattress, staring up at the ceiling.

An image flashed through Conner's mind of the midhallway collision he'd had with Elizabeth in school. He could see her nervously playing with the small heart on the silver chain that she wore every day. He could picture the way she had looked up at him like he was a bomb about to explode in her face any second—but one that she was willing to let obliterate her. How could he have told himself just weeks ago that she *understood* him? Elizabeth was as clueless as the rest of them.

Conner knew exactly how to read her tragic, sympathetic face. *You have a drinking problem, Conner. . . . I can help.*

He laughed. Oh, yeah? Well, here he was, sitting alone in his room in an extremely bad mood, with a bottle of vodka right underneath the bed—and he wasn't drinking. What kind of *problem* was that anyway?

The phone rang, and Conner stiffened. He could practically hear Elizabeth's voice, her plaintive, sad voice as she begged him to pick up and talk to her.

The answering machine clicked on after a couple of rings, and he listened to his greeting, lying perfectly still as he waited to hear her start talking.

"Hello, Conner. This is Jim Lampfield, the booking agent for The Shack." Conner sat up straight, automatically smoothing down his hair and blinking the blurriness out of his eyes. "I'm calling about the gig you played here last Friday. The management and staff were all really pleased, so I just wanted to let you know that we've—"

Conner catapulted off his bed, tripping over his guitar case as he raced to grab the phone.

" . . . got a cancellation for next week, but I need to know right away whether you can . . ."

"Hello? Mr. Lampfield?"

"Conner?"

"Yeah, hi. I'm sorry—I was just, um, taking a nap." He kicked aside the clothes on the floor as he made his way over to his desk chair.

"No problem," Mr. Lampfield said. "I don't know if you heard any of my message, but I was just telling you that we were really happy with your performance here the other night. Either you've got a lot of friends or you're a real crowd pleaser because our sales were great."

"Thanks," Conner said, sinking down on the chair.

"Anyway," Mr. Lampfield continued, "there's an opening a week from Thursday night, and we'd love to have you play again. Are you free?"

As if he wouldn't be, with an opportunity like that. "Yeah, definitely," he said, searching his desk for a pen to write down the information. "Like what time?" he asked, finally spotting a chewed-on pencil.

"Seven-thirty," Mr. Lampfield replied. "We do our shows a little earlier on weeknights."

"Cool," Conner said, scribbling *7:30 Thursday, The Shack,* at the bottom of a receipt lying on his desk.

"Great," Mr. Lampfield said. "Tell all your friends to come back. If you keep pulling in people like last time, this could become a steady gig."

A steady gig—how long had he been hoping for that?

"See you Thursday, Conner."

As soon as they hung up, Conner felt a triumphant smile slowly spread across his face.

It just proves me right—I shouldn't listen to anyone, he thought. His mom and his friends were all suddenly convinced that he was a worthless drunk. But for someone so out of control and "headed for danger," Conner was doing pretty well. He'd put on an awesome show the other night, and now he had the chance for a regular job. His hands would be fine by next Thursday—he couldn't wait to get back on-stage and play.

From now on, it was all about music for him. He'd gotten this gig by himself, and no one in his life seemed to believe that he could handle anything, so why should he bother with them?

And since there wasn't anyone worth sharing the good news with, he deserved a little solo celebration.

Conner reached under the bed and pulled out the half-empty bottle of vodka stored there. Good enough for a toast to himself.

He unscrewed the cap, inhaling the sharp scent of alcohol.

"Here's to me," he said, then took a long gulp.

Ken glanced to his left, then his right, checking out the defensive formation. He noticed that Todd Wilkins was being covered by Javier Guzman. It was a blatant mismatch—Todd was about three times faster. Coach was probably testing him to see if he was on his toes. *Come on, Coach,* Ken thought, smiling. *At least challenge me.* Ken reached his hands out under the center in front of him and called out the count.

"Fifty-nine! Fifteen! Hut! Hut! Hut! *Hike!*"

The center snapped the ball into Ken's hands, and the loud crunch of shoulder pads and helmets rang out. Ken shuffled back, keeping his eyes downfield on Matt Wells, who had cut across the middle of the field. Ken pump-faked a pass to him, watching as a lineman lunged to intercept it. Another step back and . . . there he was. Todd had cut inside on Guzman and was just about to leave him in the dust. Ken cocked back and released a high, floating ball diagonally over the middle. Todd outstretched his arms, and the ball sailed perfectly toward his fingertips . . . but he lost his footing at the last second, and the ball bounced off his hands and hit the ground.

Ken shook his head in frustration. It was a great pass, and Todd just didn't have it together.

"Come on, Wilkins!" Coach Riley yelled. "Matthews sent you a perfect pass. If you don't catch that, we won't have a chance come sectional time. . . ."

Ken glowed at the compliment. It had been so long since he'd heard the coach talking about *his* perfect passes and not Will's.

"Nice toss, Matthews," Aaron Dallas called out. Ken gave him a quick nod of appreciation.

"That's it!" Coach yelled. He blew the whistle. "Practice is over. Edelman, Ratto, you finish up your sprints. Matthews, get over here. I need to talk to you."

Ken unbuckled his chin strap and pulled off his helmet. Here it was—the big lecture. He'd actually managed to get to practice only a couple of minutes late after pulling a Superman-speed change in the locker room, and Coach hadn't said a word when he was the last player to jog onto the field. But maybe he'd been waiting until now to give it to him. Ken wiped the sweat off his brow and jogged over to the sideline.

"Matthews," Coach said as he approached. "Great practice. You read that last play perfectly. If you keep tossing the ball like that, we're a shoo-in for sectionals."

Ken's face flushed. "Thanks, Coach."

Coach Riley draped his arm around Ken's shoulder pads and started walking with him toward the locker room. "Do you know who Hank Krubowski is?"

Ken's heartbeat quickened. Of course he knew—every high-school football player who dreamed of playing on the University of Michigan's team had heard of their big scout. Besides, he'd seen the guy when he was here, recruiting Will. "Yeah, the Michigan scout," Ken said, trying not to let himself anticipate the coach's next words.

"That's right," Coach Riley said. "Well, he was at the game last week when Simmons got injured, and he called me this morning. He was very impressed by the way you handled the pressure."

"Really?" Ken couldn't hide his excitement. He stopped walking, fixing his gaze directly on the coach's face to see if he was serious.

"Yep," Coach said, standing still in front of him. "He thinks you've got a hell of an arm. And now that Simmons is out, he'd like to take another look at you." He paused, tilting his head as he stared back at Ken intently. "Krubowski's touring the West Coast right now . . . checking out some linebacker up in Washington. But he's gonna drop back by for the homecoming game and give you a closer look."

Ken felt his eyes widen. "He's coming back—just for me?" he said. The sun was beating down on him, excruciatingly hot through his sweat-soaked uniform, but he was in no hurry to get inside.

"Well, don't get your hopes up," Coach Riley said in his usual brisk tone. He looked at Ken from under his red baseball cap. "You just keep your head, and don't stop throwing those incredible passes. This could be a great chance for you, Matthews."

Ken nodded. "Right."

Coach slapped Ken on the shoulders and let a little smile peek through. "But don't start getting all high and mighty on us. Michigan's a long shot for any ballplayer."

Ken nodded, barely hearing him. He could already picture himself in that huge stadium he'd seen on television, calling out plays over the roar of a hundred thousand fans. Unbelievable.

"Matthews!" Coach said.

Ken shook his head. "Yeah?"

"Go hit the showers with the rest of your teammates."

"Right, Coach." Ken jogged toward the locker room. He felt like he was floating. Who knew that he could go from benchwarmer to college recruit in a matter of days? He'd given up on this dream so long ago.

Ken stepped into the locker room, still dazed and overwhelmed by everything he'd just heard. But as he headed back to his locker, he was intercepted by Josh Radinsky. Radinsky had blocked the walkway, and he stood there, staring at Ken with hard, cold eyes, his lips curled into an angry snarl.

"Don't you feel even a *little* guilty?" Josh demanded.

Ken blinked. "Guilty?"

Josh shook his head. "I was coming up behind you and Coach—I heard what he told you. Don't you think it's pretty sleazy to just step in and *steal* Will's scholarship before he's even out of the hospital?"

Ken felt his shoulders tense up. "Who said I was gonna—"

"Whatever," Josh interrupted. "Just don't forget how lucky you are to get this chance . . . and that right now Will's barely getting by."

Ken frowned, out of answers. Josh was right—everything good that was happening to him was only because of the terrible thing that had happened to Will.

"All I'm saying is, don't forget how you got here," Josh said. He turned and walked away, leaving Ken with a sour taste in his mouth.

Of course he knew how he had gotten here, and of course he felt bad about Will. But didn't he have a right to enjoy his own success? For some reason, no one else seemed to think so.

TIA RAMIREZ

THE WORLD IS DEFINITELY FULL OF CONSPIRACIES. THERE WAS SOME DISGUSTING MADE-FOR-TV MOVIE ON TODAY ABOUT TEEN ALCOHOLISM. IT WAS CALLED <u>BOTTLE</u> <u>HIGH</u> OR SOMETHING RIDICULOUS LIKE THAT. I SHOULD HAVE BEEN DOING HOMEWORK, ESPECIALLY CONSIDERING HOW BAD THE MOVIE WAS, BUT I COULDN'T PULL MYSELF AWAY. I KEPT THINKING ABOUT CONNER.

OF COURSE, THE MOVIE HAD AN "INTERVENTION" SCENE, WHICH WAS JUST AS PAINFUL AS I EXPECTED. IT WAS TOTALLY DRAMATIC, WITH A BUNCH OF STUPID LINES LIKE: "WE CAN'T JUST SIT AROUND AND WATCH YOU KILL YOURSELF." "LOOK AT YOURSELF, BLAKE!" "WE'RE ONLY

DOING THIS BECAUSE WE LOVE YOU." "HOW CAN YOU BE SO CASUAL ABOUT THIS?" "ALCOHOLISM IS A DISEASE. . . . YOU NEED PROFESSIONAL HELP."

UGH. EVERY TIME I HEARD THE WORDS COME OUT OF THEIR MOUTHS, I FELT SICK. ESPECIALLY SINCE I'D ACTUALLY BEEN PLANNING TO USE SOME OF THEM MYSELF.

HERE'S HOW I PICTURE THINGS GOING DOWN WITH CONNER: CONNER ENTERS ROOM. SURPRISE! ALL YOUR FRIENDS ARE HERE TO LOVINGLY TELL YOU YOU'RE AN ALCOHOLIC. CONNER EXITS ROOM.

SO NOW ALL I CAN DO IS RACK MY BRAIN FOR SOMETHING TERRIBLY CLEVER, YET KIND-OF-POIGNANT-IN-AN-ORIGINAL-WAY THING TO SAY. SOMETHING THAT WILL MAKE CONNER STAY.

YEAH, RIGHT.

melissa Fox

Life is seriously unfair. Yeah, I know you can't always get what you want, blah blah blah. But that's not what I mean. It's not fair because even when you do everything you're supposed to do, things still don't work out right.

Here's an example: You can be dating this person for years and be the perfect girlfriend, cheering him on, helping him with homework, putting up with his bad moods. You can even stick around while the person treats you like trash—cheats on you, breaks up with you for your worst enemy. And after all that, what do you get? A boyfriend in the hospital who refuses to see you.

Jeremy Aames

I know what Jade's thinking right now—she's thinking I'm a major sucker. She thinks she suckered me into hanging out with her because she looked great in that tight skirt and I'm too nice, and now she's going to make a fool of me . . . again. But she's in for a little surprise.

I can't wait to see what she does when she finds out what I have planned for us.

Jessica glanced up at the miniature fake grandfather clock resting at the end of the counter. *Only five minutes left.*

She had never been so anxious for a shift to end. She and Jeremy had been flirting all night long, first in a subtle, little-smiles way and then in a full-out, laughing-and-touching-each-other way.

Turning to her right, she saw Jeremy wiping off the other end of the counter with a moist towel.

"If you clean up that syrupy stuff," Jessica said, pointing at the gloppy mess on the glass display case in front of her, "I'll pay you back with anything you want."

"*Really?*" Jeremy raised his black eyebrows, flashing her an equally teasing grin. "Anything?"

Jessica laughed. "Except for bathroom duty," she said, nodding in the direction of House of Java's rest rooms.

"That's not *anything*," Jeremy replied. He came over and picked up a spatula, then started scraping at the cinnamon-bun icing that coated the top of the display case. Her eyes stayed glued on his strong, muscular hands as they slid back and forth with a controlled rhythm. He definitely had an athlete's hands, but luckily he had a sensitive personality to go with them instead of the obnoxious, arrogant attitude that certain other football players possessed.

Biting her lip, she checked the clock again. *Two minutes.* She had already counted the money in her drawer. All she had left were finishing touches—a couple of counter wipes and a mop-bucket dump. Everything was going exactly according to plan. She picked up the towel Jeremy had put down and used it to clean off the espresso machine.

There was no way she was going to let Jeremy leave here tonight without her. It was obvious he was thinking the same thing, but he was probably too shy to ask or too weirded out by all the stuff with Jade. No big deal. She'd suggest something friendly and innocent, like going for a walk or grabbing some ice cream.

When she finished with the espresso machine, she noticed that Jeremy was standing over by the small mirror near the minifridge, straightening his shirt collar.

"Looking good," Jessica called out.

Jeremy's face immediately reddened, and he let out a nervous laugh. He caught her eye in the reflection in the mirror, then spun around. "What do you think of this shirt?" he asked.

Jessica pretended to inspect his shirt, even though she had already memorized exactly how the soft, navy blue fabric hugged his broad chest and shoulders. "It looks great on you," she said. "Really great," she added, deepening her voice just slightly.

"Thanks," Jeremy said, his cheeks getting pink again. He looked back at the mirror and continued to play with the collar, folding it down a couple of times to try and get the exact right crease.

He wants to look perfect for me, she realized. He was as ready as she was for the two of them to get back together, and he was trying to make sure they did it right this time. It was so sweet—so *him.*

"So what's the occasion?" she asked, stepping closer to him. "Big date?"

"No," he said with a shrug. "I mean, not really." He faced her again, and she caught a strange, nervous twitch in his deep brown eyes.

Her pulse quickened as she wondered what he meant. Was he talking about her—or someone else?

Jeremy walked over to the cash register, and she waited a moment, then followed him. She stopped at the sink and pretended to wipe away crumbs, even though there weren't any there.

"So, what's that mean?" she asked to his back, keeping her voice steady. "Not really a date?"

"Well, I guess that technically, it *is* a date," Jeremy

said over his shoulder. "Not a big deal, though."

Not a big deal? Jeremy had just broken up with Jade a few days ago, and now he had another date? He was *not* the player type. She felt her temperature start to rise.

"Oh, yeah?" she responded, glad that he couldn't see her face. "Who's the lucky girl?"

"Um . . ." He paused, then turned around so they were eye to eye again. She quickly darted her gaze away from his, pressing her lips together nervously. "It's actually Jade," he muttered in a barely audible voice. "But it's *really* no big deal."

Jessica's jaw fell open. He was going on a date with Jade, after everything that happened? And he had the nerve to say it was *no big deal?* She whirled around and started wiping blindly at the spotless counter. She didn't know how Jade had managed it, but she had a feeling that all of this had come from Jessica firing her. It was her revenge. Still, how could a smart guy like Jeremy fall for it?

"Jess," Jeremy said softly. "You don't have to freak out. It's different this time—trust me."

She held back a laugh. He was way more gullible than she'd thought. She couldn't help feeling a small sting at the realization that he was forgiving Jade so easily for doing something much worse than *she* had done.

"Anyway," Jeremy said. "It looks like everything's wrapped up here, so I'm going to take off."

Jessica ducked her head, nodding. This was the moment she'd been waiting for all night long—leaving with Jeremy. But now . . . nothing was working out right.

"So, I'll see you later," he continued. She knew he was waiting for her to look at him, to reassure him that this Jade thing was okay. How exactly was she supposed to do that when it was so *not* okay?

But it was Jeremy—she couldn't leave things like this. She inhaled deeply, then pivoted, forcing a big smile. "Good night," she said.

His face relaxed into a grin, and she figured she'd been right—he did need her approval or whatever. But if he cared so much, then why was he going out with someone *else* tonight instead of her?

She watched him stride through the door, unable to take her eyes from his broad shoulders and the little curl of black hair at the back of his neck. As soon as he was gone, she threw the towel down in the sink. How had everything managed to go so wrong, so fast?

Ken stared at the image on his television in disbelief—a little boy had fallen into the baboon pit at a zoo. The baboon was walking toward the kid! The kid was squirming around like a little worm while rescue workers above plotted how to get him out.

Ken loved this show, *America's Most Stunning*

Home Videos or something like that. It was an hour of pure entertainment every Tuesday night. Of course, he should be doing homework. But ever since Coach Riley said that Hank Krubowski was coming to check him out at the homecoming game, Ken had been too excited to concentrate. He'd left a message for Maria, and he wasn't sure what was taking her so long to call him back. He couldn't wait to share the news with someone.

I just hope she actually cares, he thought. He shifted into a more comfortable position on the sofa. Maria had been acting so weird since the game Saturday night. He knew it wasn't a great move missing dinner with her parents last night, but didn't she get how much was going on with him right now? Somehow it didn't seem like she did.

She definitely understands scholarships, though, he reassured himself. There was no way someone like Maria wouldn't be psyched about a possible free ride to a great college that he never could have gotten into on grades and test scores alone.

Ken shook his head, focusing back on the adventure on TV. Wow—it looked like the baboon was trying to *help* the kid.

The doorbell rang, and Ken jerked back his head. His dad wasn't due home from work yet—and he hadn't warned Ken about any new random dates that would be showing up to wait for him.

He stood, still watching the television screen as

the baboon reached out to give the kid a lift up. He didn't want to miss the best part of the video! The doorbell rang again, followed by a shower of hard knocks.

"Chill out," Ken muttered. "I'm coming," he called, hurrying down the hall to the front door.

He looked through the peephole, happily surprised when he caught sight of Maria standing on his stoop. He could definitely skip *America's Most Stunning Home Videos* for his girlfriend.

He swung open the door, beaming at her. "Hey," he said. "I'm so glad you're here. I have the most amazing—" He stopped midsentence as he took in her expression. She was practically *scowling*—something he wouldn't have imagined possible for her. Her dark eyes were gleaming with anger, and her mouth was set into a firm, rigid line. "What's wrong?" he asked.

She brushed past him, then stormed down the hall and into the living room without saying a word. He shut the door and followed her, totally clueless. They'd already talked about dinner last night. It was all worked out. And nothing had happened since then, right? An image of Melissa Fox popped into his head, the way holding her felt . . . but he immediately shoved it out of his thoughts. He was a *guy*. Of course he wasn't immune to having a good-looking girl that close. But he didn't care about Melissa at all—not like he did about

Maria. And Maria hadn't been around to witness the hug anyway.

When he walked into the living room, Maria was standing next to the sofa, her arms folded over her chest and a fierce glare fixed on him.

"Maria, I don't know what happened, but—"

"You want to know what happened?" she cut in. "Where should I start? Let's see, okay—I was looking for my boyfriend after school because I wanted to talk to him about this football party he conveniently failed to mention, the one I'm supposed to drive him home from because he's gonna be *sooooo* drunk!"

Uh-oh. He kicked his toe into the carpet, feeling a twinge of guilt. He'd totally spaced on filling her in on the party. Well, maybe not *totally*. It was just that it had never seemed like the right time to bring it up. "Maria, I was going to tell you about that party tonight," he said. "I was going to invite you—and believe me, whatever you heard, I'm not planning on getting loaded."

He took a step toward her, and she immediately backed away, leaning against the sofa.

"Oh, I'm just getting started," she said. "So I'm walking down the hallway, looking for my boyfriend, right? I figured I could catch him before he goes into the locker room, and . . ."

No way, Ken thought, his body growing cold. *There's no way she saw.*

". . . there, in the middle of the hallway, is my *boyfriend* . . . hugging some other girl! Not just any girl, but Melissa Fox, the queen cheerleader, a girl he barely even knows. Unless I'm wrong. Maybe he knows her very well. Maybe—"

Unable to hold himself back, Ken moved forward and grabbed both of her arms just below the shoulders. "Maria, stop," he cut her off, meeting her eye. "Just let me explain, and you'll realize that it's *nothing* like you're thinking."

"There's not much to explain, Ken!" she burst out in a semihysterical tone, shaking out of his grasp. "You had your arms wrapped around her for a full minute!" She stopped suddenly, glancing around him out into the hall. "Your dad isn't here, is he?" she asked, lowering her voice.

"No." Ken immediately wished he'd said yes so he wouldn't have to hear Maria yell again.

But apparently the yelling was finished, and it was time for the worst part—the crying. Tears were rapidly filling her large eyes, and he had to resist the urge to reach out and wipe them away himself. As annoyed as he was that she was railing into him without even listening to what he had to say, he still hated to see her cry.

"Will you please let me get this out?" he begged. He rubbed his forehead, trying to get his thoughts to line up so he didn't say the wrong thing. "Melissa stopped me in the hall this morning and went off

119

on me," he began. He gave her a half smile. "Kind of like what you just did," he added. "But she made a big deal about how I never should have gone to see Will. I stood up for myself, maybe went a little too far, and then she kind of freaked out. I could tell something else was wrong, something she wasn't admitting. And I guess . . . I sort of felt responsible, you know?"

He stared into his girlfriend's normally warm eyes, searching for some light of understanding, but her gaze was still sad and . . . distant.

He sighed. "So I went to see her after school to apologize. She finally told me that Will's refusing to see her. That's why she got so mad at me. Anyway, she started crying, and I didn't know what to do so I—I hugged her, whatever. Honestly, I was just trying to comfort her. That's all."

Maria glanced away. "Do you have any idea what it felt like to see that?" she asked, her voice cracking. "I mean, Conner and Liz all over again." A couple of tears slipped down her face, and she quickly brushed them away with one slender hand.

"What?" He felt the anger start to build. "You're comparing me to that slimeball? Don't you trust me at all?"

She looked back at him, and for the first time he could see *her* in her eyes. "I'm sorry," she said. "I know you're nothing like him. But what was I supposed to think, after how you've been acting lately?

I wouldn't have thought you'd ditch dinner last night either or *forget* to tell me about some football kegger."

He took her hand and led her around to sit down on the sofa, relieved that she didn't resist. Once they were both seated, facing each other, he tried once more to carefully measure out the right words in his mind. "We haven't really been clicking this week, I know," he said, "but it goes both ways. You've been jumping all over me for the littlest things, and I have no clue why."

A strange shadow passed over her face, and she looked behind him at the hall again, as if waiting for his dad to walk right in. What was with her sudden paranoia over Mr. Matthews?

"What do you want me to say?" he went on. "The girl was bawling her eyes out—you would have done the same thing."

She bit her lip. "Maybe," she said.

"Can we just forget all this?" he asked. "It was a stupid mix-up, but it's over." He stretched his legs out in front of him, staring down at his feet in frustration. He wished he could erase this entire conversation and go back to when he'd been dying to tell her about the Michigan scout. Now he didn't even feel like getting into it—his good mood was wrecked.

"Yeah, I guess," she said, sounding unconvinced. They were both quiet for a minute. "So what about this party?" she finally asked. "Are you going?"

"The party? Oh, right. Yeah, sure. As long as you want to," he said, giving her a cautious smile.

"Whatever," she replied. "I mean, it's in your honor and everything, right? So you pretty much have to go."

"I guess so," he said. He'd never felt like this around her—like he had to watch every word he said because the wrong ones would set her off. This should have been the happiest moment of his senior year. After the earthquake, when he lost Olivia, he'd never imagined that he could be this happy with someone else and that he'd be back on top of his life—with solid grades and his old position on the football team. But it was all coming together for him.

Except for the girlfriend part, he thought, casting a sidelong glance at Maria. She'd stopped crying, and she didn't seem *mad* anymore, but something still wasn't right. And he was pretty sure that if he didn't figure out what it was—and fix it—very soon, the two of them were headed for real trouble.

Jade smiled as she stared into the most beautiful, attentive eyes she'd ever seen—light brown with flecks of green. It was easy to fall hard for this cutie.

"I hope you know how pretty you are, Trisha," Jade said to Jeremy's little six-year-old sister. She sat back against the plush cushion of the sofa. "Someday the boys are going to go crazy over you."

Trisha beamed up at her, flicking one of her long, brown braids back over her shoulder. "I think you should come play with us every week," she declared. "Are you having fun?"

"I sure am," Jade replied. She leaned toward Trisha, cupping one hand over the side of her mouth. "Don't tell your brother—but I think I like hanging out with you better than hanging out with him," she whispered in Trisha's ear.

Trisha's eyes widened, and she giggled happily. "I won't say anything, I promise," she said.

Jade glanced across the room, her gaze landing on Jeremy and his other sister, Emma. They were sitting together at the dining-room table, Emma's school books open in front of them. Jeremy was explaining some complicated math problem to her, sketching the answer out on a piece of paper.

He must have felt her staring because he paused and looked over at her and Trisha. Their eyes locked, and she smiled, enjoying the surprise in his expression. She was no idiot—it was obvious he'd planned this cozy little evening figuring she'd freak out around his sisters. He just had no idea that she happened to love kids.

Jade broke away her gaze and returned her attention to Trisha, giving her a light pat on the shoulder. "Hey, we're not done reading here, are we?" She pointed at the book on her lap—*The Shape of Me and Other Stuff*, by Dr. Seuss. Jade had picked this book from Trisha's collection because it used to be one of her favorites. She could still remember reading it out loud to her mom when her mom was teaching her how to read.

"*Just think about the shape of strings and elephants,*" Jade read, "*and other things. The shape of lips. The shape of ships. The shape of water when it drips. Peanuts and pineapples, noses and grapes. Everything comes in different shapes. . . .*"

"What are those?" Trisha interrupted, pointing at the big, tropical fruits on the page.

"Those are pineapples," Jade explained.

Trisha pointed again. "What about those?" she asked, her finger on top of a bunch of noses.

"You know what they are," Jade said. "I see one right on your face."

"Where?" Trisha asked, smiling.

Jade pretended to inspect Trisha's face, then pinched her nose. Trisha laughed, and Jade couldn't help joining her.

"Break time!" Jeremy called out. "Time for tonight's featured wrestling match!"

Jade watched as Trisha sprinted across the room and ran into Jeremy at full speed, growling. Jeremy lifted her up on his back and growled jokingly.

Jade bit her lip. She couldn't help noticing the way his biceps flexed as he lifted Trisha and also how cute the two of them were together. He probably never would have guessed that spending the night ignoring her in favor of his sisters would actually make her . . .

Make me what? she challenged herself. *Fall for him?* Jade knew better than to get attached to Jeremy—to anyone. Then she'd have to deal with all those stupid insecurities and jealousies. Did Jeremy *really* like her? How much? Was he still attracted to Jessica? Jade didn't want to deal with all that stuff. As long as things stayed fun—like playing with kids, kissing, and getting revenge on Jessica—then everything was fine. But anything past that was *trouble.*

"The Baboon is down!"

Jade looked up at the blissful, strained smile on Jeremy's face as Trisha hung from his neck, pulling on his ear. Emma slapped him on the hip and laughed, and Jeremy glanced over in Jade's direction, giving her a quick wink. She grinned back, crossing her arms over her chest and leaning back against the sofa. Yeah, Jeremy was cute. He was fun. But he was still *temporary.*

They all were.

Jessica Wakefield

Could guys be any more gullible?

Take, as a completely random example,
Jeremy Aames. He's an honor-roll student,
and he is <u>not</u> a dumb guy. But some good-
looking girl comes along, flirts a little, and he's
totally gone. Then he <u>finds</u> her cheating on him.
(He might have had a certain someone's help,
but that's not important right now.) So <u>why</u>
would he go out with this totally unfaithful
girl again?

And I <u>don't</u> want to hear it's because he
really likes her.

Evan Plummer

I have been sitting here doing the most pointless thing in the world—trying to figure out what to say at Conner's intervention.

"Sorry, man, but we think you're an alcoholic."

"I really hate to do this."

"Whatever, man, you might as well check out Alcoholics Anonymous just in case."

The more I think about it, I can see that there was no reason to keep coming up with stupid things to say. I won't have to say anything. Because Conner's gonna walk right out the door.

We may as well start planning option B.

CHAPTER

Big Break

"I have to admit I'm impressed," Jeremy said. He finished washing the last dish in the sink and placed it on the drying rack, then turned off the water. "You're great with kids," he added.

Jade smirked, balancing herself against the kitchen counter. Emma and Trisha were settled in front of the television in the living room, watching some happy animal movie. And she was finally alone with Jeremy—which, as much as she liked his sisters, was something she'd been looking forward to all night.

"I don't get why you're so surprised," she said. "Trisha's adorable, and she reads all the books I used to read. Like the Curious George and Amelia Bedelia ones. I love that stuff."

"I guess I was kind of expecting the whole plan to catch you off guard," he admitted with a shrug. He walked over to the oak kitchen table and sank into one of the chairs. "You know, bore you out of your mind to see if you wanted to stick around for the real Jeremy Aames."

129

She pushed off the counter and followed him over to the table, sitting across from him.

"I wasn't bored at all," Jade said, actually telling the truth.

Don't forget your purpose here, she reminded herself. Sitting up straighter, she reached out and started playing with the empty glass napkin holder. "It was kind of nice getting to relax tonight since tomorrow I have to hit the pavement, looking for a new job."

Jeremy licked his lips, staring down at the table. "Yeah," he said. "That sucks." He paused, then looked back up at her. "So what exactly happened at House of Java anyway? I can't believe that Ally didn't give you any kind of warning before she fired you."

Jade feigned her best confused, shocked expression, letting her eyes widen just the right amount. "Ally didn't fire me," she blurted out. "Jessica did."

"What?" He focused his gaze on her intently, his mouth slightly open. "*Jessica* fired you?"

"I—I figured you knew that," she stammered. This was *perfect*. "Jessica told Ally that I skipped work that time and that I'd been coming in late a couple of shifts, so I guess Ally had Jessica fire me."

"I can't believe that." Jeremy shook his head.

Jade hesitated. As much as she'd love to rip

Jessica Wakefield apart for his benefit, she knew it wasn't the right time.

"It wasn't Jessica's fault," she said. "No reason to kill the messenger."

"But she didn't just give you the news," Jeremy said. He stood up and started pacing along the floor, as if this was just too much to accept. Good—he needed to learn what his precious little Jessica was really like. "I mean, she's the reason Ally wanted you to leave," he said, almost to himself.

"Well, yeah," Jade *reluctantly* agreed. She let go of the napkin holder and clasped her hands in front of her. "But she's an assistant manager. Maybe she felt like she had to report me."

"Whatever," Jeremy said. "She could have said something to you first instead of going right to Ally. This is crazy."

Jade, 1; Jessica, 0. Wait. Jessica had fired her. They were tied—but not for long. Jade sighed. "I'll find something else," she said. "Hopefully soon."

Jeremy came back over to the table, standing in front of her with his lips pressed together. "Listen, I want you to know that I'll help, okay? This—This shouldn't have happened," he muttered, a strange expression on his face. It was like he was blaming himself, not just Jessica. "Okay?" he repeated.

She nodded, observing the deep furrow in his brow. He was really upset—even more than she'd expected. Well, it was just because she was so good at this. And because he was such a nice guy too.

Such a nice, cute, predictable *guy,* she thought.

Ken watched intently as a fly crawled across his kitchen table. He raised his hand above the scurrying creature, ready to catch it with one swooping motion. But he stopped, putting his hands back in his lap. It wasn't like the fly was hurting him. He just needed to get out his aggression on *something.*

If he'd seen Maria hugging some guy in the hallway, he would have walked right up and found out what was going on. Why hadn't Maria done that? It was like she didn't even trust him enough to confront him right then and there. What did that say about them?

Yeah, so he hadn't told her about the party. Big deal—it was some stupid jock fest that meant nothing to him. And it shouldn't have meant so much to her.

Ken pounded his knuckles against the table, and the fly immediately shot up into the air and flew away.

Because of all that stupid stuff, he hadn't even been able to share his news with her—the most exciting thing that had happened to him in so long. *Even if we hadn't been fighting, would she have cared?* he wondered. Maria was the one who had given him the guts to go back out there and rejoin the team in the first place, but that was when he didn't get any real minutes on the field. She didn't want to hear about football—it didn't mean anything to her.

Ken heard a soft scraping sound in the hallway—his dad's slippers. He held his breath, hoping the slippers weren't headed for the kitchen. He'd managed to avoid the big father-son chat so far tonight since he'd been shut up in his bedroom when his dad came home.

"Hey, Ken," Mr. Matthews said as he walked in the room. Ken let out his breath in a sigh. "How did practice go?"

"Fine," Ken said, not looking up from the table. Could his dad be any more predictable? Not, "How was your day?" or, "How's Maria?" but, "How was practice?"

"Is the coach giving you a good workout?" Mr. Matthews pressed. He went over to the refrigerator and pulled out a bowl of grapes, then brought it with him over to the table and sat down across from Ken. "Not putting any extra strain on the arm, are you?"

"No," Ken said, glancing up at his dad. Mr. Matthews popped a couple of grapes in his mouth, then held out the bowl to Ken. He shook his head.

"Now, I remember you used to run a lot of plays in the shotgun formation last year," Mr. Matthews continued through a mouthful of sloshing grapes. "Has Coach Riley let you practice that?

133

Because I think it could really work. You've got a couple of fast, slippery receivers . . . and you've got such a great arm." He shook his head, then beamed at Ken. "I can't wait to see you in action again," he added.

Did Mr. Matthews take some kind of loving-parent pill? He was a completely different person than the one Ken had been living with all these months. But as angry as he was about all of that, he still couldn't help being happy to have someone in his life actually *get* what the game meant.

"Yeah, we've been working on the shotgun a little," Ken said. "It's always been my favorite formation."

Mr. Matthews smiled. "I wish we'd used that system back when I was playing ball. . . . That would have made the game a lot more exciting."

Ken shifted in his seat, wondering if he was about to make a huge mistake. But he just couldn't hold this inside any longer. "Hey, I have some news, actually," he blurted out. "Coach pulled me aside after practice and said that Hank Krubowski, the Michigan scout, is swinging back in town for the homecoming game. I guess he liked what he saw the other night," he finished, feeling his cheeks redden slightly.

"No kidding!" Mr. Matthews said. His impossibly wide grin somehow managed to get even bigger. "That's excellent—this could be your big break, son."

"Yeah," Ken said. "I guess so."

Mr. Matthews shook his head. "You have really pulled it together," he said. "I know I gave you a rough time for a while, but it was just because I knew you had so much natural ability, and I hate to see that wasted." He paused, his eyes narrowing slightly. "I'll be at that game too, so make me proud, okay?" He stood, giving Ken a pat on the shoulder before putting away the grapes. "Good night," he said as he headed out of the kitchen.

"Good night, Dad," Ken answered.

He listened to his dad's footsteps trail down the hall, then lifted a hand to rub his forehead. He'd promised himself that he wouldn't give his dad a second chance. But he had to admit, it was nice to be able to talk to someone about football. And maybe his dad was telling the truth—and all that abuse he'd been doling out was his twisted way of trying to take care of his son.

At least Mr. Matthews acted like he cared that something good was happening to Ken. Right now, he couldn't say the same thing about his girlfriend.

Elizabeth paced back and forth in the living room, clutching the portable phone in her hand. This was crazy—since when was calling Conner such a huge deal?

Stupid question. Since his mom informed her that her boyfriend was an alcoholic—that's when.

She stood still, taking a deep breath. Then she held the phone up to her ear and pressed the speed-dial button with Conner's number stored. The quick succession of beeps started, and she immediately jammed her finger down to hang up. Why did it have to dial so fast?

Her heart hammered in her chest, and her fingers were sweaty as she gripped the phone tighter.

What was she thinking anyway? He wasn't going to answer. He never did anymore. And another message on his machine wouldn't help anything. She needed to go see him—right now. She knew she was supposed to wait, to hold off until the intervention, but how could she? Tossing the phone onto the sofa, she ran over to the hall table by the front door to grab her keys. Jessica had the Jeep, so she'd have to take her mom's car.

She slipped the key ring over her finger and stood there by the door, listening to the keys as they jangled together.

What if he was drunk? What if she got there and he was so wasted and out of control that he—

No, that's not who he is, she told himself. Conner would never hurt her. Not physically, at least.

She swung open the door and came face-to-face with . . . a reflection. Jessica was standing there, her arm outstretched as if she'd been about to open the door from the outside.

"Hey," Jessica said. "Nice timing." She paused, scrunching her face together. "Where are you going? It's late."

Elizabeth's eyes darted around, not meeting her sister's. "Um, I was going to head over to Conner's," she muttered.

"Oh, no, you're not," Jessica declared. She stepped inside and took Elizabeth's arm, dragging her back into the living room. "There's no way I'm letting you go there after everything you've told me," she said. "Just sit down a second, okay?" She guided Elizabeth over to the sofa.

Once they were sitting, Jessica reached up to brush a few strands of blond hair out of Elizabeth's face, fixing her with a concerned sisterly gaze. "Are you holding up okay?" she asked gently.

Elizabeth sighed. "Not really," she admitted. She'd told Jessica all about Mrs. Sandborn's visit and the planned intervention, but she knew that her sister still didn't totally *get* all of this. She barely did herself.

Jessica tilted her head sympathetically. "Have you talked to him?" she asked.

Him. Elizabeth flinched. Whenever a relationship started to get bad, all your friends would start calling the guy *him* instead of using his actual name.

She shifted uncomfortably, rubbing her hands together in her lap. "We ran into each other in the hall today," she said. "But he bolted. Big shocker."

"So . . . what about the intervention?" Jessica prodded. "When is that?"

"I don't know." She paused, staring down at the floor. Every inch of her dreaded the whole

137

thing—standing there and facing off with Conner, knowing that within seconds he'd be furious at her, maybe never even speak to her again.

Not like things are much better now anyway, she thought.

"I know I'm not a big expert on this stuff," Jessica said. She sat forward, her blue-green eyes wide and serious. "But it sounds like it's getting pretty bad, and I can tell you're about to lose it. So maybe you should just get this thing over with. What are you guys waiting for anyway?"

Elizabeth shrugged. She started to pick at a loose thread hanging off the sofa. "Me, I guess," she finally said. She was pretty sure everyone was waiting on her word, and she *knew* Mrs. Sandborn was anxious to set everything up.

"Well . . . then do it," Jessica said. Sympathy was practically oozing out of her pores, and she scooted closer to Elizabeth, as if worried that she couldn't sit up on her own.

I barely can, she realized. Her sister knew her better than anyone, and maybe Elizabeth didn't always take her advice, but this time it was hard to ignore. She was falling apart in a major way, and it was time to do something about it.

"You're right," she said. "I'm going to call Conner's mom right now—we'll do the intervention tomorrow."

To: tee@swiftnet.com
From: lizw@cal.rr.com
Re: Intervention

Hey, Tee,

   I know you're as freaked out as I am, but we just have to get it over with. I talked to Mrs. Sandborn, and it's set up for tomorrow night. Can you let everyone know to show up at his house around seven-thirty? I don't really feel like talking about this with anyone else right now, and if I write to them, they'll probably call me.

   Thanks,

                         Liz

Conner McDermott

Once upon a time, there was a boy who didn't speak. It wasn't that he <u>couldn't</u>—in fact, Ronald Biddlewinks had excellent vocal equipment. A strong tongue, round, forceful lips, and a violent voice box.

But Ronald Biddlewinks couldn't see what everyone was talking <u>about</u>. Everyone— his parents, teachers, kids on the playground—they were always chattering, making nonsense sounds and responding with more nonsense. But despite his parents' many lectures and bribes and forced reading sessions, Ronald had no interest. He preferred to watch the way the sun glimmered on the rippling water at dawn, to hear springtime leaves laughing, and to gorge on the honey from his father's backyard beehives.

Because he refused to talk, Ronald Biddlewinks's first friend was made of wood. From the moment they met on Christmas morning, Ronald and Woody the Guitar have spent every day together. They do not communicate in "words" as we know them, but in Music—a language in which they are both fluent. Woody taught Ronald how to sing without opening his mouth, how to capture the meaning of things with a simple strum of the strings. Not nonsense talky sounds, but sounds like the laughing leaves. In turn, Ronald taught Woody to loosen his strings a little, to stop vibrating all the time and mellow out, to sit and appreciate a microscopic parade of little black ants.

Ronald Biddlewinks toured the countryside with Woody tucked under his arm. In every village and nook his concert turned into an all-night party of dancing and drinking and feats of derring-do. He was treated as a celebrity. And yet when the concert ended and dozens of shapely young women rushed at Ronald, frenzied by the palm wine, he would say nothing. He smiled, but the fair maidens soon became disenchanted with Ronald's silence and scattered.

One night, at a show in the province of Bettelmie, Ronald had a life changer. That is to say, a thing happened that snapped Ronald into reality. It was a beautiful woman. Not beautiful in the regular sense of luscious lips and endless curves, but Inside Beautiful, such that she poured out all the right things.

When Ronald Biddlewinks saw this wondrous creature, his mind became fixed. Fortunately, his hands knew the song well enough to play on autopilot. So Ronald played on, staring at this woman, the muse of his life, and his song went into a place that he had never known existed. His fingers massaged Woody's strings like possessed angels, forming a melody so beautiful that the entire crowd moved as one huge, entranced animal.

That's when it happened. Ronald Biddlewinks began to sing.

They were the first sounds he'd ever uttered besides the occasional yawn, belch, or hiccup, and they were . . . absolutely beautiful. They were not words, 'tis true. Ronald's singing was more like sublime grunts, lions' roars, and begging, hopeful cries. They were directed at the short-haired, long-nosed, gray-eyed girl in the back row.

In less than a fortnight Ronald and Ms. Back Row entwined themselves as Mr. and Mrs. Biddlewinks. Unfortunately, Ronald soon learned that Mrs. Biddlewinks was not what he had thought she was. She wanted to change him, to suffocate his music. And so Ronald again became silent, although the paparazzi claim to have caught him "murmuring" and "mumbling" to his agent.

The only press release Ronnie's agent has ever given contained just one insight into Ronnie's mysterious existence. He said: "My only true companion is my best friend, Woody Guitar."

CHAPTER 10
No Coming Back

"Baby! All the ladies got their eyes on you . . . baaabay!"

Ken turned his car onto El Dorado Drive, singing along loudly to the cheesy R & B song playing on his radio. He turned up the volume, beating out the rhythm of the music on his steering wheel.

When he and Maria had first heard this song, they'd made fun of it together. He smiled as he remembered that night. The song had come on in the car on their way home from Crescent Beach, and he'd thought it was so cool that she could make him laugh like that.

That was just a couple of weeks ago, he realized, turning the radio back down. He'd never imagined they'd be so far apart so soon. Ken glanced out the window at the store windows as he passed by, noticing the little flower shop on the corner.

That's perfect, he thought, easing down on the brake for the red light. He would get Maria some flowers later to show her that she was on his mind all the time—not Melissa or anyone else.

He bit his lip. He was actually wondering how Melissa was doing, but it's not like he was seriously *thinking* about the girl—not the way he thought about Maria, his girlfriend.

Ken heard a honk from behind him and looked up into his rearview mirror. A Jeep packed with people was coming up quickly, and the driver seemed to be waving at him. The car honked again, then switched lanes and pulled up to the left of Ken. Now that they were right next to him, he could recognize his teammates Aaron Dallas and Seth Hiller, sitting up front with a bunch of good-looking girls piled in the backseat.

Ken laughed, then rolled down his window. "What's up, Dallas?"

"Matthews!" Aaron responded in a half roar. "You psyched for tonight?"

Ken nodded, even though the party was pretty much the last thing he cared about right now.

"Hey, you were awesome in the game Saturday," one of the girls in the back called out over Aaron's shoulder. She flashed him a grin that exposed perfect, gleaming white teeth and flipped her long, red hair over her shoulder.

She's flirting with me, he realized. It had been happening a lot this week—random cute girls coming up and saying stuff like that, stuff about the game. It's not like he was available to go after any of them—or even wanted to—but it was kind of cool suddenly being so in demand.

"It's gonna be *ridiculous* tonight," Aaron said. "I hope you're ready, man."

Ready? It did sound like they were planning a majorly wild event. Ken didn't say anything, and just then the light turned green, so he gave the guys a quick wave, then rolled up the window and accelerated.

Maybe a crazy party was just what he and Maria needed, he thought as he cruised down the road. A chance to relax from all this heavy stuff that had been going on lately. He'd buy her some flowers—some *roses*—and then spend the night showing her how much she meant to him. And once things were on track, he'd tell her about the scholarship too.

It's ridiculous to think she wouldn't be excited about that, he told himself. Maria was acting weird lately, but even if she wasn't into football, she was into college—and Michigan was a great one.

Ken turned the radio up again full blast. Everything was going to turn around today; he could feel it. He was back on top of his game, the big Michigan scout was interested in him, and he had an amazing girlfriend. He wasn't going to let anything bring down this mood.

Jessica wandered into her first-period history class, her mind still foggy from lack of sleep. Her alarm hadn't gone off this morning, so she hadn't even had time to shower before dashing to school. Then the traffic on River Road from some minor accident made her and Elizabeth late for home-room. And now she had to deal with spending an entire class period in the same room as her two favorite people. No, wait, Will Simmons was still out, so that meant it would just be—

"Hey, Jessica!"

Ouch. There's my alarm. Jessica spun around, almost losing her balance. Jade was marching toward her, wearing another of her ridiculously short skirts with a crisp white shirt and *way* too much eye makeup.

Great. As if this day didn't already suck enough.

"Hey," Jessica replied, narrowing her eyes suspiciously. She pulled her books against her chest, as if they could somehow protect her from her new enemy's death glares. Although actually Jade was grinning at her like they were still good friends.

Jade sauntered over to an empty seat next to where Jessica was standing and sat down, stretching her perfectly thin legs out in front of her. "So, no hard feelings about the House of Java thing, okay?" she said.

Jessica frowned. Something was up. She sank into a chair behind Jade and dropped her books down onto the desk in front of her. "Yeah, sure, no hard feelings," she muttered. *Now that you've managed to snap Jeremy back up,* she added silently. She picked up her pencil and started turning it around in her hands, noticing that the eraser was worn down almost all the way.

Jade swiveled to face her, and Jessica wondered why she could possibly want to prolong this conversation. She glanced over at the doorway hopefully, but no teacher in sight. Never when you *wanted* them to show up.

"I mean, it was just a little dose of bad karma, right?" Jade pressed. Jessica noticed that her black hair was practically gleaming, while her own hung limply against her face, probably giving her zits at this very moment from the unchecked-grease factor.

"And that's fine," Jade continued, "because I've already gotten some great karma in return."

That's where this was going. How could Jessica not have realized sooner? It was definitely gloat time for Jade. So all she had to do was make like Jeremy meant nothing to her. Yeah, no problem there. At least she was a good actress, right? She kept twirling the pencil, resisting the urge to smash the nice sharp point right in Jade's face.

"It's *totally* helped my relationship with Jeremy," Jade gushed. She was still smiling, but there was something hard and defiant in her black eyes, something that made it obvious how badly she was trying to make Jessica hurt. God—the girl really *hated* her.

"I think we just needed some time away from HOJ and that whole *scene,* you know?" Jade said, her voice getting louder.

Impulsively Jessica did her Will search, then remembered that he wasn't there. Even after everything that had happened, she didn't want Will—or his witch girlfriend, Melissa—to think that she had lost a guy to Jade.

"Anyway, I guess working together made things a little weird because last night I was over at his house—you know, hanging out with his sisters and then some alone time later, and it was like we were closer than *ever*."

Jessica felt her teeth scrape together, and she practically snapped the pencil in half. Jade couldn't care less about Jeremy—she was doing this to get revenge on her. The worst part was that Jeremy would just end up getting hurt all over again.

"So, you know, I guess I should say thanks," Jade said. "Obviously you had no idea when you fired me." She paused, letting the words dangle there for a second. "But you really played a *big* part in us getting back together." She flashed one more triumphant, taunting smile, then flipped back around to face the front of the classroom, leaving Jessica simmering.

If there weren't so many people around, she probably would have ripped into her right now. But that was what Jade wanted—to see Jessica react. She wasn't going to give her the satisfaction. She wasn't going to let Jade know that everything she'd just said had done exactly what she'd intended—completely ruined Jessica's already terrible day.

* * *

"I heard everyone on the football team has to do ten shots of tequila. . . . This party's gonna rock!"

Maria winced as she heard the words over the other hallway noises of slamming locker doors, shuffling feet, and random chatter. So Ken was going to be downing tequila? She glanced at Andy, who was waiting beside her while she finished getting her books out of her locker. "If I hear one more thing about this party," she muttered, "I'm seriously going to throw up. I can't even believe I'm going."

Andy's dark red eyebrows shot up. "You're more ticked off than I thought," he said. "Why don't you just tell Ken you don't want to go to the stupid party?"

She sighed, staring into her locker without really recognizing any of its contents. "Because we need to have fun together," she replied. "There was—some stuff happened yesterday, and it got pretty bad." She paused, wondering if she should tell Andy about the Melissa moment. Somehow she just didn't have the energy.

Shutting her locker, she turned back to face Andy again. "I want to do this tonight, for him," she explained. "But I'm not really sure if I can handle a bunch of beer-guzzling idiots." *Especially if my boyfriend becomes one of them.*

"Well, you'll be showing up at the party late

anyway," Andy offered. "Maybe you'll miss the worst of it."

Maria frowned. "Late? Why?" She shifted her backpack up onto her shoulder, glancing down at her watch. Again Ken was a no-show for their typical locker catch-up.

Andy scrunched up his face in confusion. "Because of Conner," he said, like it was superobvious. "You're not skipping out on the intervention, are you?"

"What do you—that's tonight?" she demanded. She hadn't talked to Elizabeth at all last night. Actually, Tia had called, but Maria hadn't picked up the phone because she'd just wanted to be alone.

"Yeah, around seven-thirty," Andy said. He scratched his head. "I figured you knew."

"No, I'm glad you told me. You know what—I bet when I tell Ken that's tonight, he'll want to bag on the party anyway. I mean, who knows how long this thing will take?"

"I'm guessing just long enough for Conner to see us and then turn around and leave," Andy said, sounding unusually dark. In fact, he'd been rather short on the quick-witted jabs lately. Maria made a mental note to follow up on the stuff he'd said yesterday, about feeling like no one was really there for him right now. She'd just been so wrapped up in all this Ken stuff.

But now I don't even have to worry about the

party. It's not like she was using Conner's problem as an excuse or anything, but he and Elizabeth needed her for something big. There was no way Ken wouldn't understand that.

"Hey, speaking of your man, he's coming up behind you," Andy told her in a low voice. "I'm going to take off. I'll see you there tonight, though, right?"

"Yeah, of course," she promised before Andy began to speed walk off down the hall.

Right away Maria felt two muscular arms encircle her waist from behind. A warm body pressed against her back, and she inhaled the combined scent of deodorant and cologne. Maria let out a small, happy sigh, then turned to face Ken.

He was smiling down at her, his blue eyes free of all the resentment they'd seemed to direct at her last night. "What was his hurry?" he asked, nodding in the direction Andy had zoomed off in. "Did I scare him away? Don't tell me he was trying to move in on my turf," he teased, his arms still loosely draped around her.

Maria laughed. "You're on to us. Andy and I are having an affair. It doesn't even matter to him that I'm, you know, the wrong *gender* and all."

Ken stiffened, squinting at her with a puzzled expression. She took in a sharp breath as it hit her that she'd never actually told Ken about Andy. So much else had been going on, and she hadn't really thought it was her place to fill him in. But somehow just now she'd assumed he knew anyway. Obviously he didn't.

Maria instantly reached out to grab his hand, keeping her gaze directly on his. "That just slipped out," she said, glancing around to make sure no one else was in eavesdropping distance. Most people had already cleared out of the hall on their way to class. "I'm sorry I never told you or anything, but Andy's—"

She stopped, noticing that the blood seemed to be draining from Ken's face as his skin got paler and paler by the second. "I think I've got it," he said, swallowing.

So then what was the problem? He looked *upset*. Yeah, maybe it was a bit of a shock, but it wasn't anything bad. Unless Ken was one of those people who . . .

No, not Ken. Not my incredibly sensitive, caring boyfriend. Not possible.

Ken cleared his throat. The color was starting to come back to his cheeks, but he was staring down at the floor now, scuffling the floor with his right foot.

"Ken?" she prodded, feeling a lump rise in the back of her throat. "Is there some kind of problem?"

"No," he answered right away, looking up to meet her eye. After a moment he glanced away again. "I mean, there's nothing *wrong* with it, I guess."

"You *guess?*" Maria snapped. This couldn't be happening. Not here, in the middle of school, with the bell about to ring any time now.

"Look, I'm sorry—I'm not good at saying the right thing, okay?" he said. He shoved his hand through his hair. "I just don't really know how this stuff works, that's all."

The bell finally rang—blaring loudly for what seemed like an eternity. Maria's eyes didn't move from Ken's nervous, tightly drawn face.

"We can talk about this later, right?" Ken said, forcing a weak attempt at a smile. "When I pick you up for the party or something. I'll be at your house around seven." He leaned over and planted a quick, awkward kiss on her cheek, then dashed off.

Wait, her mind screamed as she watched him fly down the hallway. She hadn't had the chance to tell him about Conner's intervention. *It wasn't exactly the best time anyway*, she reasoned.

By the time he showed up at her house later, he would have had a chance to process the stuff about Andy, and he'd probably feel so bad about acting like a jerk that he'd have no problem ditching the party. Besides, maybe he'd been different this week, but he couldn't have changed so much that he wouldn't see how Conner's intervention meant much more than a football party. She wasn't certain of a lot right now, but she was sure of that.

*   *   *

Work from home and be your own boss!

Jade groaned, then threw the newspaper back down on her kitchen table. In her experience, if the classified ad seemed to promise too much, it usually wasn't for real. Last summer she had taken a job with youcouldactuallybeyourownboss.com and ended up doing "data entry"—when she wasn't busy stuffing envelopes.

Jade picked up the paper again and scanned the rest of the page.

Prime-time restaurant seeks food servers, she read. Yes! Then she saw the name of the restaurant: First and Ten. They'd already fired Jade once. . . . That was probably enough.

Frustrated, she balled up the whole page and threw it across the room. This was hopeless. She had no recommendations and no excuse for having lost two jobs in the past several weeks.

Crossing her arms over her chest, she scowled at the crumpled paper lying on the tiled floor. Then she stood and walked out of the room, leaving the newspaper where it was. She could practically hear her father's lecture over the phone about "responsibility" and "initiative." Worse, she could picture the tense expression on her mom's face when she found out Jade had screwed something up yet again.

She was on her way to her bedroom when the doorbell rang. *I am not in the mood to deal with some annoying salesman,* she thought, figuring she'd just pretend she wasn't home. But curiosity pushed her to walk through the living room over to the apartment's front door. She stood on her tiptoes to peer through the peephole, and as soon as she saw who was standing there, a huge smile spread over her face. The one person she could actually deal with right now—Jeremy!

She quickly unlocked the door and yanked it open, relieved that she hadn't changed into her lounge-around clothes yet.

"Hey!" she greeted him, instantly realizing that her voice had too much enthusiasm in it. *Tone it down,* she thought, letting her smile fade a little.

Jeremy smiled. "Hey, Jade." His red, button-down shirt hung loosely off his broad shoulders, not tucked in, over a pair of khakis that nicely accentuated his long, muscular legs.

"So . . . can I come in?" he asked.

She laughed. "Yeah, of course," she said, stepping back so he could walk around her. She closed the door behind him, then led him over to the couch and plopped down next to him.

"I'm so glad you stopped by," she said, rubbing her palms along her knees. "I was just about to freak out over my total lack of job options. According to the *Sweet Valley Tribune,* I am a worthless, unemployable waste of space."

Jeremy shook his head. "I know the feeling," he said. "When I was checking around for other stuff, I couldn't find anything decent." He paused. "Actually, that's kind of why I'm here. I thought you might be having a tough time, so I wanted to let you know about a job possibility."

Jade bit her lip. A new job was great—but she'd been hoping Jeremy was here because he couldn't wait to get her alone after last night's little "playing-house" date. She'd been exaggerating just a little to Jessica this morning when she'd made it sound like she and Jeremy got hot and heavy after they finished entertaining his sisters. In fact, the night had been pretty tame. But there was no reason for Jessica to know that—especially since Jade was sure that she and Jeremy would get there soon enough anyway.

Jade inched a little closer to him, letting her hair fall over her face so that it was almost touching his shoulder.

"What kind of job?" she asked, keeping her expression blank.

"My dad knows this guy," he said, "a friend from high school who's opening up a new sushi restaurant downtown." He reached into his pocket and pulled out a scrap of paper with an address scrawled across it, then handed it to her. "I already told him about you—I mean, you know, that you have experience as a waitress and everything."

Jade smiled, recognizing the shy note that had just come into his voice. "That sounds great," she said, folding up the piece of paper. "Thanks a lot, really. I'll stop by tomorrow."

She reached over to place the paper on the edge of the sofa, then turned back to him, making sure to position herself even closer so that they were just inches apart. "And I think I know how to show my appreciation," she said in a low voice. Then she leaned forward and pressed her lips to his, gently at first, then slowly increasing the pressure until they were engaged in a full-on serious kiss.

Jeremy moved his hands behind her back, pulling her to him, and the tiny hairs on the back of her neck tingled at his touch. He was by far the best kisser she'd ever experienced.

She started to feel like she was sinking into him, losing her grasp from the amazing sensation of the kiss, so she pulled back a little, catching her breath. She looked into his unbelievably sweet eyes and blinked, trying to keep back her emotions. This was crazy—it wasn't like her to feel so . . . so *swept away*.

"Thanks," she whispered, licking her lips. "For the job, I mean." Jeremy was a great guy, but she was going to have to be very careful not to let herself get carried away. Because something told her that if she actually fell for Jeremy Aames, there would really be no coming back.

Ken Matthews

I know it's supposed to be a really horrible thing these days if you're actually <u>not</u> okay with everything everyone does. And honestly, I don't care if someone's gay—I mean, it's not that I think it's bad or wrong or whatever. But I've never known anyone who was gay before, and it's just a little weird to suddenly find out that this guy you've hung out with tons of times was into <u>guys</u> all along.

No, I don't think that means Andy wants to jump me or anything stupid like that. It's just . . . I don't know. I wish Maria didn't make me feel like a major jerk for not being instantly fine with the whole thing when no one even told me all this time.

COUNTDOWN . . .

6:30 P.M.: Conner, going crazy in his room, decides he'll go practice for his gig at the beach. His mother doesn't stop him, but tells him sternly that he must be home for an "extra-special family meal" at eight.

6:33 P.M.: Elizabeth lies on her bed, fully dressed, thinking about Conner. She realizes how much their relationship has changed since the day they first met, when they both thought they knew exactly what the other was about—and then found out they were totally off. She realizes that this could be the day that everything changes between them forever.

6:47 P.M.: Evan checks the Web site of Alcoholics Anonymous, hoping for some help with his intervention plans. Its suggestions would seem appropriate for anyone but Conner McDermott.

6:48 P.M.: Andy looks at a letter Conner wrote him in eighth grade. It ends with the line: *I'm exactly the kind of punk that high-school kids will want to pummel next year.*

7:02 P.M.: Tia bursts into tears in the shower.

7:15 P.M.: Maria checks her watch, nervous. If Ken doesn't show up soon, they'll be late for the intervention.

7:22 P.M.: Elizabeth and Tia arrive at Conner's house at the same time. They sit down with Megan and Mrs. Sandborn, and the four of them can't come up with anything to say to each other.

7:48 P.M.: Andy and Evan arrive together.

7:53 P.M.: Conner, burnt out from his jam session but dreading the "extra-special" part of this "family meal," finally packs up his guitar and gets ready to head home.

8:00 P.M.: Knowing that they have plenty of time to prepare (Conner never shows up when he says he will), the crew has talked about everything *but* tonight's main event.

Ken held the rose behind his back as he walked up the steps to Maria's front door. He had wanted to get a whole bouquet, but he'd been running so late that he just had time to grab the rose from one of the vendors on the street on his way here. Still, he'd heard that a single rose was actually very romantic. He just hoped Maria agreed.

Straightening his shoulders, he reached up with his free hand and pushed the doorbell, listening to it reverberate through the Slaters' house. He was so relieved that after all the fighting and awkwardness lately, he and Maria finally had a chance to just go hang out and chill, have a good time together. Maybe he would even have a couple of drinks like the guys wanted, just to celebrate himself for a little while. He deserved it, right?

He heard the shuffle of approaching footsteps, then the door opened and Maria stood there, still wearing the jeans and peasant shirt she'd had on at school today. He'd thought maybe she would have changed for the party, but it didn't matter. She looked beautiful no matter what she wore.

"Hey," she said. "Listen, there's something I—"

"Wait," he interrupted, wanting to start the night off right. He brought his hand out from behind his back and held out the rose to her.

Her eyes widened with that perfect combination of surprise and happiness, and she took the rose gingerly in her hand, leaning down to sniff it. "This is . . . thank you," she said, smiling up at him. She hesitated, then stepped forward and gave him a light kiss, a reminder of what he'd missed so much these past few days. He was about to move closer to deepen the kiss, but she pulled back.

"The rose is great," she said, "but we really have to go."

Ken frowned. Now Maria was in a hurry to get to the party she'd been all freaked out over?

"I mean, we have to go to Conner's house," she explained, leaning against the door frame.

Ken felt his stomach sink with a heavy thud. Conner again—he knew he wasn't going to like this.

"Liz is having the intervention tonight," she continued. She glanced down at her watch, and a worried crease appeared on her forehead. "In fact, it's starting any minute now, and the whole point is for everyone to be there together so Conner knows we feel the same way. He really needs all of us there."

Us? Ken's heartbeat accelerated. Why did

McDermott need him? And why did the guy need *his* girlfriend?

"So are you ready?" Maria pressed.

Ken gave his head a small shake, trying to understand what was going on here. Maria had just *decided* they were going to this intervention thing instead of to the party in his honor—and she hadn't thought to give him any kind of heads up? First she dropped the Andy bomb with no warning, and now this.

Ken shifted his weight from one heel to the other. "Maria, I barely know Conner. And what I do know is how much he messed you up. How are we supposed to do any good there?"

"Well—we would really be there as added support. For Elizabeth too," she added. She was still holding the rose, gripping it more tightly.

Ken couldn't believe she was doing this. They finally had a chance to hang out and relax, to enjoy the fact that he was being rewarded for all those weeks on the bench, and she wanted him to go sit at her ex's house instead to watch some big, intense confrontation where he'd be totally out of place?

"You're not seriously thinking of not *going,* are you?" she demanded, her frown deepening. "Because we have to. I promised Liz, and . . ." She trailed off, probably seeing the flashes of anger in his eyes.

She'd promised *for* him, without even asking?

"Did you consider checking with me first?" he asked through clenched teeth.

"We can do this later," she said, putting the rose down on the ledge next to them. "Right now we have to get over there. Okay?"

Ken exhaled slowly, staring down at the welcome mat. No, it wasn't okay, and he was worried that if he looked her in the eye right now, he'd really lose it. She was asking for way too much here. He'd just come out of the hardest time in his whole life, and she knew that better than anyone. Now that things were finally turning around for him, all he wanted was for her to share his *happiness* the way she'd comforted him through all that messy stuff. Why was that so difficult?

"Ken?" she said. "Hello? You are coming with me, aren't you? You're not going to stand here and tell me that some party is more important than saving our friend's life."

He let out a snort as the rage grew stronger. For her to sink that low, after what he'd been through with Olivia . . . Yeah, he knew that a human life was far more precious than a million parties. He knew that in the most painful way possible. But this wasn't about saving Conner—it was about Maria trying to nose into something that she knew nothing about instead of putting Ken, her boyfriend, first.

He steeled himself, then raised his gaze to meet hers. "No, I'm not going," he said.

"What?" Her voice came out in a half squeak, and he could see the hurt in her eyes, but right now he didn't care. No, he cared—but there was nothing he could do. She'd made her choice, and it wasn't him. So now he had to make his.

"I'm not going," Ken repeated. "The guys planned a party tonight for *me*, and I wanted you to be there by my side, celebrating the fact that I'm finally getting my life back. But maybe you don't want to be a part of that life anymore."

She jerked back her head as if he'd slapped her, and he felt an instinctive desire to take it back, to reach out to her. If she would just tell him he was wrong, that she *did* care, that she was happy for him . . .

"Maybe not," she responded in a tone so cold he barely recognized it. "Maybe this just, I don't know, isn't working."

Not working. Was she—were they breaking up here? The knot in his gut tightened, but he wasn't about to back down.

"Okay," he said lamely, unsure how to respond. He didn't want this to be happening, but it was like he was standing back watching the whole thing, powerless to stop it.

"Okay, then," she said briskly. "So have fun at your party." She slammed the door in his face, leaving the rose lying there on the ledge. He stared at it for a second, then grabbed it and crumpled the petals, tossing the remains into the yard.

This was insane. She was dumping him because of Conner McDermott. Maybe she really wasn't over the guy after all.

Whatever, he thought, ignoring the tightness in his chest. He stormed back across the yard to his car, making sure to stomp hard on the rose as he walked by. She wanted him to have fun tonight? That's what he would do. He'd go hang out with people who could accept Ken the quarterback for just who he was. Which obviously didn't include Maria.

Maria Slater

Just because you find out your boyfriend is totally different from who you thought he was doesn't mean you can ditch your best friend when she needs you most. So Ken and I are over. Fine. I still have to go to Conner's house and help with the intervention. I still have to . . .

Stop crying.

Elizabeth stared down at the palms of her hands as if she'd never seen them before. Sweaty lines and sticky grooves going every which way, curving out from underneath the thumb up into her forefinger. It was as if they didn't belong to her at all. They were just these trembling body parts that happened to be attached to her.

Trying to prove she was still in charge of herself, she balled her hands up into fists. Obviously they were *hers* if she could control their movements, right?

What if Conner never shows up? Where's Maria? What if he shows up dead drunk and unable to speak? What if he storms out and never speaks to me again? Andy said Maria was coming, and she's never late. The thoughts raced each other in her mind, tumbling over each other.

She glanced over at Andy and Evan, who were having a quiet conversation in the corner, their heads bent together. They were probably discussing what an idiot she was to ever try to set this up, how Conner would hate them all. She tore her gaze away from them and searched out Mrs. Sandborn, who was perched on the edge of the sofa next to Megan, looking like all she wanted to do was run out and chase Conner down to drag him here herself. She caught Elizabeth's eye and forced a smile, which came off more as a kind of halfhearted grimace.

"Are you hanging in there?" she asked.

Elizabeth nodded. "Yeah, I'm okay," she lied.

"It's okay to be nervous, you know," Mrs. Sandborn said. She came over and rested a hand on Elizabeth's shoulder. "I was hoping that you would, well, *initiate* the intervention. Someone has to speak for the group first, to explain to Conner that we're all here because of him, that we're not against him." She pursed her lips. "I'm afraid that if I initiate, Conner won't respond at all. You may be the only one he'll listen to."

I don't know about that, she thought. Conner hadn't listened to anything she'd said recently. But she knew his mom was counting on her. "Sure," she agreed. She glanced over at Tia, who was sitting at the other end of the sofa, tossing the green throw pillow over and over in her hands. "I'll do it," she said.

Mrs. Sandborn sighed. "Good. Thank you, Elizabeth. For all of this."

She nodded again, feeling like all of her movements were suddenly detached, the way her hands had seemed just a second ago.

"So, Tee," she said, raising her voice to get her friend's attention. "Do you know what you're going to say yet?"

Tia kept looking down at the pillow in her lap, but Elizabeth could tell from the expression in her eyes that she'd heard her. "I don't know," she said quietly. "I guess I'll just follow your lead."

There was a strange note in her voice as she said it, almost like the way she'd sounded back when there was all that tension between them over Conner. Did Tia feel like she should be the one leading this whole thing?

Maybe she should, Elizabeth found herself thinking. She was desperate for whatever would help her boyfriend, even if it was someone else and not her.

"What was that? It sounded like someone pulled in," Mrs. Sandborn said. She jumped up and ran over to peek out the curtains.

"Is it him?" Evan asked.

What do I say? Elizabeth racked her mind for the words but couldn't come up with anything. She'd spent every hour this week preparing for right now, but it had gotten her absolutely nowhere.

I just want you to be happy. . . . You're an alcoholic. . . . We know you think this is stupid. . . . It's a disease. . . . You know deep down we're right. . . . You know how much I love you, Conner.

Her heart squeezed inside her chest as she focused her eyes on the front door of the house. This was it. If she messed up, every person in that room would suffer for it. But most of all, Conner would.

"False alarm," Mrs. Sandborn said, her voice flat. She let the curtains fall shut again. "It's just Maria."

Conner turned down his street, feeling the familiar sense of dread as he approached his house. Dinner with his paranoid mom wasn't something he was looking forward to, but hopefully if Sandy was

174

around, then Mrs. Sandborn would know better than to start tossing out more crazy accusations.

He pulled his Mustang into the driveway, then glanced in his rearview mirror, doing a double take when he noticed a bunch of his friends' cars all lined up farther down the block. There was Andy's gigantic vintage Caddy, Maria's green Taurus—and Elizabeth's Jeep.

Conner let the engine idle while he decided what to do. His first instinct was to take off, but maybe he should get this over with. Whatever they were doing there, he needed them to get the message to leave him alone for good. This was a fine time to do it. He reached into the backseat and pulled the almost empty bottle of vodka out of his backpack, taking a couple of swigs. Let them think he was drunk if they wanted. Even better.

He would just walk right in there, tell them off, and head on up to his room and lock the door behind him. It seemed like a decent plan.

He turned off the car and made sure to slam the driver's-side door extra loudly so they'd know he was on his way. Then he sauntered up to his front door, almost looking forward to the chance to get all these annoying do-gooders off his back.

Show time, he thought as he pulled open the door. He walked through the short hall into the living room, surprised to hear only heavy silence, no rushed, frantic chatter. But when he stepped into the room, they were all there. His mom, Tia, Elizabeth, Andy, Evan, Maria, and . . .

Megan. Fury coursed through him at the sight of his little sister sitting close to Elizabeth on the sofa, staring at him with wide, scared eyes. How could they have brought her into this? How *dare* they?

The silence was interrupted by the sound of his name, coming out in the softest, quietest tone he'd ever heard. But he could still recognize the voice, and his eyes went right to Elizabeth.

She met his gaze, her blue-green eyes filling rapidly with tears. "Conner," she repeated, louder this time.

His breath caught, and emotions he hadn't thought possible flooded his body. But the anger was stronger than anything else. She had betrayed him in the worst possible way. They all had—everyone in this room. He tore his eyes away from hers and stared down the rest of his friends, trying to make his absolute loathing clear. If they wanted to stage a stupid little confrontation for him, fine. But Megan was here. And that was too much—way too much.

He balled his hands into fists, feeling his face grow hot. Then he spun around and started to head for the door.

"Conner—wait," Elizabeth blurted out. He turned, not quite looking at her. Let her say whatever she had to say, and then he'd be out of there.

"Conner," she said, "we're here because we love you."

JADE WU

8:06 P.M.

Yeah, finding me a job was sweet.
And yeah, he's an amazing kisser. All
right, fine, he's a great kisser who chose
me over Jessica Wakefield. Big deal. It
does not mean that I am falling for
Jeremy Aames.

KEN MATTHEWS

8:15 P.M.

Okay, there's no way that Maria and I really broke up tonight. Because two people who like each other that much don't just <u>break up.</u> Unless . . . unless they really aren't right for each other in the first place.

ELIZABETH WAKEFIELD

8:22 P.M.

We're here because we love you. How could I mess up like that? _I think I just made the worst mistake of my life._

CONNER MCDERMOTT

8:22 P.M.

This isn't happening. I refuse to believe this is actually happening.